JIGGER BUNTS

Center Point
Large Print

Also by Max Brand® and available from
Center Point Large Print:

The Cure of Silver Cañon
The Red Well
Son of an Outlaw
Lightning of Gold
Daring Duval
Sour Creek Valley
Gunfighters in Hell
Red Hawk's Trail
Sun and Sand
The Double Rider

**This Large Print Book carries the
Seal of Approval of N.A.V.H.**

JIGGER BUNTS

A Western Story

Max Brand®

CENTER POINT LARGE PRINT
THORNDIKE, MAINE

This Circle Ⓥ Western is published by
Center Point Large Print in the year 2019 in
co-operation with Golden West Literary Agency.

February 2019
First Edition

The name Max Brand® is a registered trademark with the
United States Patent and Trademark Office and cannot be
used for any purpose without express written permission.

Printed in the United States of America
on permanent paper.
Set in 16-point Times New Roman type.

ISBN: 978-1-64358-099-9

Library of Congress Cataloging-in-Publication Data

Names: Brand, Max, 1892-1944, author.
Title: Jigger bunts : a western story / Max Brand®.
Description: First edition. | Thorndike, Maine :
    Center Point Large Print, 2019. | Series: A Circle V western
Identifiers: LCCN 2018052011 | ISBN 9781643580999
    (hardcover : alk. paper)
Subjects: LCSH: Western stories. | Large type books.
Classification: LCC PS3511.A87 J54 2019 | DDC 813/.52—dc23
LC record available at https://lccn.loc.gov/2018052011

Editor's Note

While it was believed that all the Western stories Frederick Faust had written had been published in some form, a number of stories set in the West were recently discovered among his unpublished works. The two connected stories appearing here were among them.

PART ONE

The Man Who Never Was

Chapter One

Enough time has gone by to make the telling of this possible, I guess. Although you never can be sure, and as old Doc Lawson used to say: "Where there has been a shooting, the best thing is to keep your mouth shut and act as though nothing had ever happened."

Doc was probably right. He had a way of being right.

But what keeps me from following his advice here is partly because these things happened such a while ago that by changing names I don't think that I'll be stepping on sore toes. And partly I think that I have to tell it because I want to get it off of my conscience. You can't have a thing like this eating in you for long years without wanting to talk about it. Confession is what a man needs, and confession is what I've never had a chance to have. Until now.

Because suppose that I step out and say to some of my friends: "Look here, till this and this happened, long ago . . . what do you think of the part I played in it . . . and how wrong was I?"

Well, my friend is apt to say: "If you were lowdown enough to ever do a thing like that, you're a good deal too lowdown for me to take any pleasure in knowing you right now."

And a man can't afford to shuffle the spots off of his friends. Particularly when you get to my time of life. Along about when a fellow is twenty years old or a bit more, friends are luxuries, you might say, because he's so full of ginger and so willing to take what's coming to him in his life that friends don't seem to matter, particularly. But you shake along to the other side of seventy and see how many different slants come into your head! I have got about five real friends, now, but if you were to offer me a million dollars in cash for each one of them, I would only sit down and laugh.

However, this confession had to be made.

And since I didn't want to lose myself any friends, I thought that I might as well try the stuff with queer names in print and let the readers vote on how wrong I was.

Because I know that I was wrong. It's only a question of *how* wrong.

But I'm going to leave you to decide that for yourselves.

Chapter Two

To start right in at the beginning.

My job was sort of straw boss to what we'll call the Bar L outfit. Or rather, I straw-bossed the gang that ran the Bar L cows in the north all winter long. Which was about as raw and mean a job as I ever tackled in my life.

I can locate the place for you in a general way by stating that it was up near a reservation, and when I tell you that most of the redskins on that reservation were Sioux, I suppose that you can work out for yourself about which reservation I mean.

Or, if you want any further location, I could tell you that it was part of the country where the ground was all ripped apart and plowed up by the rains, when they came. And where trees didn't thrive particularly; the soil was that mean and clayey.

All summer, it was dust that swarmed all over you and crawled down your neck and fair choked you. And all winter it was mud. God-awful mud! Mud that collected together. Mud that was cemented with glue. So when you put down your foot most of the country tried to stick to the boot when you tried to lift it. Mud so bad

11

that when the snow heaped up and then battered down flat and hard, it was a mighty relief. Mud so mighty bad that we used to hate the coming of spring because it meant the thaw, and the end of the snow, and that wet, soaked, sticky ground— billions of tons of it all hankering to get onto your shoes or your clothes and dry off inside of your shack.

So by this you ought to know about when this happened, and also with half an eye at any old map, you could tell about where.

When the fall came along toward the close, and the sky got blacker and blacker and the clouds blew lower and lower with a wet feel in them that you have in your lungs and on your skin before you can understand, we all got pretty mournful, because we knew that pretty soon part of us would have to travel north and start in on that job which we hated.

The Bar L outfit worked out a scheme like this.

It ranged cows right alongside of the reservation lands. And of course it wasn't supposed to range cows *on* the reservation lands. But a few would be bound to mix over. That was natural. And a few of the reservation cattle would be bound to mix over on *our* side of the line, and everything was just the way it should be, and nobody could find any fault because cows have got a natural way of wandering when the feed gets poor or when the wind is blowing hard and long.

But the Bar L outfit beat that game all hollow.

The reservation lands were cracking good ones and there was pasture that would have made the mouth of any cattleman water. And what was to keep the Bar L from just drifting a few more thousands onto that reservation, and then a few more thousands still?

The Indians didn't care much. All winter long, an Indian is interested in almost anything more than in how his cows are getting along in the snow. He likes to sit inside and swap lies unless his belly gets so empty that he has to take in his belt a lot of notches.

In the old days, the Indians used to get out and raise the devil now and then in the winter. We figured it that they had a reason behind what they did, because they wanted nothing so much as lots of chuck and lots of sleep in the cold weather, and when they went on the rampage, we knew it was because some rascal of an Indian agent had been cheating them out of nine-tenths of their provisions. Which was what happened all the time.

However, that didn't make them any better neighbors. It was like living on thin ice all the time. You never knew when that ice was going to crack and let you through to Kingdom Come.

In the meantime, here we were drifting the Bar L cattle in on the reservation lands as fast as we could.

And when the spring came—or maybe it was in the autumn—along would come an inspector or two, sent out by the government to count the cows to see whether or not the avaricious cattlemen were taking advantage of the poor Indians by using up their pasture.

Well, that was always a funny performance.

Mostly those inspectors were honest men. But they didn't know any more about cattle than they did about the man in the moon. You'd think that wouldn't keep them from being able to count brands. When you start out and have to travel around a circle for five or six days, you begin by being very conscientious. But after a while, you get tired of riding up and looking at the brand, and you ask the cowpuncher along with you if those are new cattle, or ones that they've already counted on the other side of the range. And then the honest cowpunchers ride out and take a look and they come back and tell you that those cows had already been counted on the far side of the range and that with the wind where it is now, the cows are bound to do a lot of drifting from one part of the range to the other.

Well, sir, I've seen inspectors go out and look fifty thousand cows fairly in the eye and come back and write a conscientious report that they had seen only five thousand. And willing to swear by what they report. And willing to fight for what they've said. Because a man hates to think that he has been made a fool of.

If it hadn't been that there is this element in our human nature, I would not have to make this confession now!

Let that go for the present.

You can see by the layout as I show it to you that we had a nasty job on our hands, up there in those bleak badlands. And about the only chance we had to liven things up was when we had a whack at pulling the wool over the eyes of those inspectors. And we did that not because we were particularly devoted to the Bar L, or because we disliked the inspectors, but simply because it is a lot of fun to make a fool of the *other* fellow. Which ties right in with the other half of what I've just been saying.

However, it takes a lot of swallows to make a summer, and there weren't enough inspectors in the business to give us a happy time and keep us amused at that camp. And every autumn it was harder and harder to get the boys to stick it out and volunteer to tackle the job.

I had a new crew nearly every season for that work. And it was hard work that needed experience. I got fifteen dollars a month extra, which was enough to sweeten the work for me. Besides, I was boss, and a man likes to have a little responsibility. I knew that the men who ran the Bar L didn't give a proverbial damn about me, but still it was sort of nice to have the running of that little batch of men and that great big batch of cows every winter.

The bosses let me do everything and even order all the provisions, except the bacon. They had their own bacon which they used to buy wholesale, and they used to get a firm that managed to raise hogs that were all fat and no muscle at all. That bacon was a mighty disgusting lot of stuff. It was just white grease and there was no way of slicing it up or cooking it that would make it anything *but* white grease. And a poor article of bacon is a bad thing to feed to cowhands in a camp where bacon simply has to be the biggest thing in the diet. However, I could put up with the diet. And once we got into camp, I could do everything exactly as I pleased. I could fire and hire. Which is about all the authority that you can expect to have placed in your hands by any outfit. And away out there, seventy miles from anything that had the nerve to call itself a town, being kingpin of the gang was quite an inducement.

However, what was an inducement for me was no particular inducement for any of the others. And, as I've said, every year we had to make up a new bunch to take north for the winter work. We had to give up all attempt to get experienced hands. Anything that was willing to ride bucking horses and eat that filthy bacon was good enough to be called cowpuncher in my camp.

And that was how I came to hire Jigger Bunts.

However, since he is what my confession is about, he deserves a new chapter off by himself, I suppose.

Chapter Three

He came in at the end of the time that I had laid
out for the hiring of my crew. And if I hadn't been
desperate, I should not have taken him because I
could see at one look that he was the awkward
age of boys. That is, he was about eighteen.

When a boy is eighteen he is sure to be all
wrong. Either he has a bigger body than he knows
what to do with, or else he has more head and
less beam than he needs. He's sure to be out of
proportion. He's got to the age when he doesn't
fall down stairs any more, but he just falls into
scrapes all the time.

You see, he can't understand the right place
for himself. Where he should really be is off at
a school somewhere along with the other young
lunatics about his same age. Or if there's war,
you'll find that he's at the front. Somebody told
me that a third of the soldiers in the Civil War
were sixteen years old or *under* that age.

Well, if there has to be a war, I suppose that the
Army is a good place for a boy about that time
of life. Because he doesn't know what to make
of himself. He's got his full height and within a
few pounds of his full weight and within a jump
or two of his full strength. If he gets tired a little
quicker than a grown man does, he gets rested

a lot easier. And he has this advantage—that no matter what sort of a load he carries on his back, he never carries nothing on his mind. Mentally, you might say, he is always in light marching order.

He has a goal, yes, but that goal is just to find a good time, no matter where he has to look for it. Also, he wants to find out everything that's worthwhile in the whole world, and he can't rest until he's got to it. He doesn't want any delays. Make him sit down in a corner for five whole minutes and he'll up and start a revolution. Put up a fence, or a mountain, and tell him that he can do anything that he wants except to climb over that fence or that mountain, and right off there is nothing that he really wants to do and nothing that puts any sauce in life, except to climb up that mountain and stand on his head at the top of it.

Yes, doing what he's told not to is his idea of perfect happiness. And even when he *does* try to do something right, God has planted in him an instinct for doing it wrong. Or, if you take it the other way, he has an instinct for doing wrong things the right way.

Same time, you can't put him in his place the way you can with a little boy. Nothing makes him fire up more than suspecting for a minute that he's not being treated as respectfully as a man had *ought* to be treated. Because being a man is a new job with him, he's like a cow on a new range—got to go sniffing around in every corner of the new place and show fight whenever anybody puts a hoof nearby. That's the way with a boy. If you just smile at him, he feels that he's morally dead to all honor unless he ups and hits you on the chin.

I had seen quite a bit about boys, and I could remember pretty clear when I was a boy myself. So I knew that hiring an eighteen-year-old was most likely laying out work for two grown-up men.

However, I was already two men short. And the winter had all the signs of being a whopper. The beavers were laying in great big stores, and the dogs had coats about twice as thick and silky as they had had the year before. So we all knew that we were in for a mighty bad season up there on the edge of the reservation lands. Also, if the bad weather started working hardships on the Sioux, *they* were apt to start running amuck. And all of these reasons dovetailed in together most beautifully, so that I only had to look at a man to make him turn and look the other way.

All I could get were some fellows so old and so tough that they didn't care what happened to them. Most of them had been anything you're pleased to name, from coal muckers to sailors before the mast. And two of them, by my own knowledge, had worked on big square-riggers.

Those were the days, you understand, when the

sailing ship was having her last classy fling at the world, and the square-riggers were howling around the world with their decks half under water all the time, and the skippers standing around with guns in their hands, threatening to shoot the first man that dared to let go a rope to shorten sail. And a man who had sailed under a skipper like that was ready for almost anything.

After laying out on a yard and reefing in a sail that was covered stiff with a solid inch of ice, hanging onto the yard with his teeth and reefing the sail in with both hands and both feet—after doing work like that, around the Horn, a man didn't really mind nothing else. And even a winter up there doing the work that we had to do was sort of a party.

By those two specimens, you can judge the rest of the gang that I had hired. Most of them had raised so much ruction in the world that they were pretty glad to get off there where nobody was apt to hear of them for a while. And they were so hard that they didn't even talk, mostly. They would just sit around and think, and every man's face was a study. You could see that they were chatting with themselves and their past.

They were so hard, that though I had lived all my days out where the boys grew like iron, I used to wake up in a sweat, dreaming bad dreams, all that winter long.

At any rate, when I saw the sort of material I

had to work with that season, and the boy came along and said that he heard I wanted men and that he would be *glad* to work for me, I just looked him over and grunted to myself. As I've said, I knew that a boy at that time of life can't help being no good to anybody, beginning with himself. But I had to have him—and so I took him. And I couldn't help asking him why he *wanted* to come out and work for me, and if he thought that maybe my camp was a sort of winter vacation trip for invalids.

As cool as you please, he stood up there and he looked me in the eye and he says to me: "I know that it's a hard life, but I'd consider it an honor to serve under a man like you, Tom Reynard."

I thought that he was sure joking, of course. And I tried to smile in sympathy with the joke, which is always a lop-sided smile when you know that the joke is on you. I wanted to knock him down, of course, but I held myself back.

I was in my late thirties myself. That is to say, I had a sense.

"You are a great joker, I see," I said to him. "And what might you be driving at?"

"Oh, I'm not joking at all," he said. "But I've heard all about you, Reynard! And I've heard about your Indian fighting, too."

I give him a pretty straight look. My Indian fighting was something that the boys all sort of enjoyed laughing about, from time to time.

Because, about five years back, some of the boys with the devil in them, trailed me back from town when I was headed toward the ranch that I was working on, and they rode all bunched over in the saddle, like Indians, and pretty soon they came whooping at me.

I got down and shot my horse and used him for an earthwork and opened fire on them. And while they were charging in and charging back again, I fired about fifty bullets at them. The dark came on, and after I had waited there until I was about frozen, I dared to start off and I got to the ranch the next morning and found that the story had got there ahead of me. It was one of those jokes that are too good to be true, and what those boys told about the straightness of my shooting and the way I lay behind my horse was enough to make a whole county hold its sides laughing. So you can guess that my best friends never mentioned the word Indian without looking me in the eye.

This kid went straight on, though, and his face was as serious as a book.

He said: "I've heard how you held off forty Sioux and killed seven of them! And I want to say, that I don't see any reason why that shouldn't be written down and published all over the world. People ought to know about that wonderful thing that you've done, Tom Reynard!"

He said it with a lot of emotion wobbling back in his throat. The same sort of a voice that the hero has in the play, when he says to the father of the heroine: "I will stick by you to the end, until death do us part, Mister Smith."

Or maybe you don't go to that sort of a play?

Of course, when he said that to me, I figured that the young rascal had a sense of humor, which is a pretty rare equipment for a boy of that age to have, except in the line of horseplay. And still, it's a hard thing for a man to appreciate the laugh on his own expense, and I was about to out with something nasty when I saw Sam Mitchell at the other end of the hotel porch looking pretty innocent.

I shifted part of the blame onto Mitchell the minute I saw that look on his face. I said to the boy: "What's your name?"

He said: "Bunts is my name, sir."

"Leave off the sir," I says. "Mostly I am called Reynard . . . or plain Tom. What is your front name?"

"Jeremy," he said. "But at home I am called Jigger a good deal of the time."

I said: "Jigger, if you want to work for me, report to me tomorrow morning and we start out. I'll be glad to have you."

He got a red, happy look on his face, as if I had presented him with a chunk of gold and a title. Then I got away from him and went to Sam Mitchell. I asked him what the devil he meant by talking to a tenderfoot that way.

"Tom," said Mitchell, "there is some that are born foolish and that study most of their lives to improve on what nature made them, and this boy is one of the lot. He came out here with a lot of book talk in his head about Indians, and such. Also, he wanted a hero, and I didn't see anything wrong about making you fit the part. All I did was kill seven Sioux for you."

There was nothing I could do except to tell Mitchell what I thought of his sense of humor, and then I went on my way. And the next morning, when I gathered up my men for the trip out to the ranch, there was the boy, nickname and all, looking as happy as a lark. So we started out.

Chapter Four

I had to prepare the boys for the foolishness of this fellow. And on the way out I got a chance to drop a word in their ears.

I said to Jigger Bunts: "Jigger, we got to watch ourselves in this part of the country. And you might ride ahead and keep a look-out, and if you see any sign of Indians, you come pelting back to us."

Jigger turned pale with happiness. It was as though I had knighted him or something foolish like that.

"Yes, sir," he said, "I'll do my best." And he galloped away.

Of course, there was no danger of any trouble with Indians just then. They had been pretty well flogged by the United States cavalry in the past two years, and all they wanted to do then was to rest up for a year or two and get ready for more mischief. So, when Jigger rode on ahead, the boys all looked a little queer at me, as though they thought that I was drunk.

I told them right away just why I had done it. I gave them about as much idea of Jigger as I had gathered from him and from Mitchell the day before. Jigger had come from some place in upper New York state, I think it was. And he had

26

been raised well and he was pretty well educated. But times were too dull for him back there and he had come along to this part of the world where he could have a chance to do something that might interest a man.

I told them, too, about the famous Indian fight in which I had stood off forty Sioux and how I had killed seven of them. That brought a pretty big laugh from the boys, and no wonder. Now and then you hear wonderful things about what a white man, particularly one of the scouts, used to do to the Indians. Most of all when they were alone.

And it is mighty queer that they usually *were* alone when they did their most heroic and wonderful fighting. There was never a witness to tell about it. According to some of those scouts— who were a lot of them just tramps that were too lazy to be regular cowhands or hunters—one white man could clean up no end of redskins. But observing is all on the other side. One red man was all that any one of the boys I knew wanted to have on his hands, and yet I knew some pretty tough characters. Maybe the Indian wasn't much account when it came to a pitched battle, though even there you'll find if you read the accounts that he gave Uncle Sam's best cavalry some tough times of it, but when it came to small parties, they were certainly poison for the whites that came in their way. And as for me or any other man holding off forty Sioux and killing seven of them during the game—why, it's the straightest sort of nonsense, of course!

So the boys had their laugh, but I warned them that they had better not laugh at me when Jigger was around, because the first thing that he would want to do would be to fight on my account!

And Jigger was not the sort of a boy that you would want a fight with. He had black eyes just about as bright as polished steel, and he had a fine supple pair of shoulders with a crease down between them in the back that made a wrinkle in his coat all the time. And he walked on his toes, and he had nice long arms, and the cords of his wrists were as big as hamstrings. The boys had noticed these things, too. And of course they didn't want any hand-to-hand trouble with Jigger, any more than I would have wanted it.

But they had started a game as soon as they got to the ranch and they kept it up all the time. The game was to make me out a wonderful sort of hero and tell all sorts of exaggerated stories about the things that I had done. These stories were always told when Jigger was around, of course.

It didn't make any difference what they said; Jigger was willing to believe anything. And while some wild, stupid yarn was being told, he would turn those big black eyes of his over to me and worship me and admire me in a style that used to make me feel pretty hot.

Of course, that was simply raw meat to those wolves that worked for me. Their joy was in listening to one of those crazy stories and watching Jigger's face and mine, and then to swallow all of their laughter. They used to sit around with stony faces and let out little exclamations and shake their heads as if they were full of wonder. And every one of them would be curling up inside and fairly dying with laughter.

You'll wonder that they could have kept it up all winter long without any break. But I assure you that they would have done it without a break. It was the bright spot in their lives. And they used to come in with a hungry look in their eyes every night, ready to sit around and swallow up some more mirth.

And the result was that they were bubbling all the time. It was nothing to see one of my men, in those days, riding through the snow or the mud and fairly rolling around in his saddle and busting with laughter. And nobody around to sympathize with what he was laughing about.

And every one of those men went around with a sort of wise look that was mighty irritating to me. And there was always a laugh to be seen around the corners of their eyes.

However, I stood for it for a long time because the work was being done on that ranch in a style that it had never been done before, and the cows were getting the finest care you could imagine, and there were no glum, silent places in the evenings.

Silent evenings are the worst poison that you can feed to working men. Give the fellows a chance to stretch and laugh—or just talk—after the day's work is over, and they'll forget all about sore muscles, and bad chuck, and blistered hands, and monotony, and everything. But when they begin to sit around in the evening in silence, then you know that you have trouble ahead of you, and pretty soon there is going to be fighting, or sulking, or grouching. And then the complaining starts. And for my part, I would rather be on a starvation party than on a party where there are a lot of grouches along.

However, there was a time when I couldn't stand the gaff any longer. They worked me up beyond what you might call a saturation point. And I was beginning to worry, too. Because every evening it seemed impossible that that young fool could sit there and swallow the lies that that gang made up. Not polished lies. Just rough, raw lies. The rawer and the cruder they could make them, they liked it all the better. Because the fun was to see the tenderfoot swallow them.

Of course, that fun wouldn't have amounted to anything if the boy had been as stupid in every way as he was in this one way. But take him all in all, he was a mighty exceptional youngster.

I've told you what I thought about boys of eighteen and how they have a natural talent for doing things in the wrong way. But that Jigger Bunts was an exception. There was hardly a way in which he showed up as a tenderfoot after he had been on the ranch for a month.

In the first place, before he came out West, he knew a lot about horses. He had ridden them ever since he was a little youngster. And there was no fear of them in him, and of course that was a great thing. He rode as well as any old hand in the party, and more than that, he *liked* to try the bad horses. Inside of a week, he had all the worst outlaws in the outfit on his string, and every morning it was a sight to see one of those devils performing, with the kid sitting up straight in the saddle and laughing and enjoying it, and beating the bronco with his hat and slamming his spurs into him, and quirting him plenty. Half a dozen ridings took the gimp out of most of them and they began to act pretty reasonable, but a few of his string were mean and stayed mean all the time.

He was a handy boy with a rope, too. He had been dreaming about the West and the Western ways for years, and for years he had been working with a rope back there in his own home. I don't mean to say that he was a roping expert, but after he got the hang of a rope, he could do his day's work alongside of any one of us.

31

Well, a man who can ride and who can rope has a pretty fair start as a handy man on a ranch. But he needs to know a lot more, and that boy was ideally suited for picking up knowledge. He had his eyes open all the time and he had his ears open, too. And no matter what drivel the boys talked to him in the evenings, when they had him out on the range during the day, they saw to it that he heard nothing but sense, because they knew perfectly well that clumsy work on his part could simply put more on their own shoulders.

The results were fine. That kid with his bright eyes that were never still had seen nearly every-thing on the range in the first month, and by the time the snows began heavy and bad, he was a good deal more use than anybody else because he was never tired, and he was never proud. I mean he was always ready and willing to do anything that he could for any of us. Most kids of that age, as I've said already, hate to have anybody take advantage of them, but Bunts was not that way at all.

Take him in the bunkhouse. He would sit over in a corner mending a bridle, maybe, and you could be sure that it would be somebody else's bridle and not his. There he would sit with his bright black eyes snapping as he took in everything that was said and never a word would come out of him except just an exclamation, now and then.

And all the time it was: "Hey, Jigger, reach me that Bull Durham, will you?"

Or: "Kid, rouse up your stumps and grab that paper for me, will you?"

Or: "Looks like the woodbox is getting sort of low."

You never had to ask twice. He would bounce up and get what you wanted, and he would do it with a smile, and when the woodbox was empty, he would always slide out through the door and come back with his face and hands red and blue with the cold outdoors and his arms full of wood.

Any of you who have been in camp can guess what a mighty lot of comfort it was to have a boy like that around.

But all the time I sat back and said to myself that this was too good to be true, and that no matter how well the kid was acting now, sooner or later he was sure to bust out and in one wallop do enough harm to put him in the class where all the eighteen-year-olds belong.

I only wish that I hadn't been such a sure-fire prophet.

Chapter Five

Well, it was my own fault.

If I had let things go along as they were, we never would have had any really bad trouble. But things got to such a point that I *couldn't* stand it any longer, and I want to tell you how it happened that I kicked over the traces. I want to tell you the whole scene, so that you'll have an idea of just what I was going through.

To give you an idea, too, of how everything was hitched onto me and my wonderful actions, I can say that it started like this.

One of the boys said: "Was any of you ever in Boston?"

"Sure," said Charlie, who was one of the square-rigger sailors. "I went all the way from Belfast to Boston that time when I saw Reynard fight forty-eight rounds with that Englishman in the ring."

He makes a pause here. And I see that I am in for another grilling. They have made me almost everything else. They have made me a great prospector, and Indian fighter, and lumberman, and hunter, and everything else, except the skipper of a ship. And now they are going to make me a great prize fighter, when I've never had more than two fistfights in my life.

I'll admit that that was roughing me a bit. But I set my teeth and endured it all.

"Who was that Englishman, now?" says somebody to me.

I answered that I didn't know.

The kid had been holding onto himself all this time and now he broke out: "Jiminy, chief, have you been a prize fighter, too?"

I said nothing.

There was a sort of unwritten law that no matter how the game went, I should not have to affirm any of the crazy things that the boys invented about me. They had to carry along for themselves. And while I sat there, frowning down at my cigarette, Charlie, the sailor, chipped in and shouted: "Has he been a fighter? *Has* he been a fighter? Why, good Lord, boys, the kid don't know that Tom has been a fighter!"

And he put back his head and began to laugh. And all the other boys were very glad, of course, to have a chance to laugh too, and they fairly raised the roof laughing at me, and at the kid, and at the wonderful joke, and at the good time they were having. While I naturally got a little hotter than usual.

There was something about that—I don't know what—that made me mad.

I said: "Look here, Charlie, and the rest of you, quit it! I'm tired of being made the . . . ." I stopped there, just in the nick of time.

And the kid jumped up and said: "Why, chief, it's only because they admire you so much! You don't think it's anything else, do you? Of course, there isn't a man here, I guess, that would dare to make a joke out of you."

He stood up there with his black eyes blazing and his jaw sticking out like a rock. And not a soul let out a whisper. And I didn't blame them, either. I would as soon have invited a wildcat to drop down my back as get into trouble with that boy.

No, they all sat around as solemn as owls. Because, of course, what he said simply played into their hands more than ever.

"Make a joke of him," said someone. "I guess not. Back in the days of my youth, when I first come sashaying out this way, maybe I would've been that foolish. But I've learned since not to take no liberties with a two-gun man. Not me."

And they all sat about and shook their heads, very solemn.

Now, it didn't need anyone with the intelligence of a child to know that I wasn't a two-gun man. In the first place because I was never better than a fair average with a revolver—that is to say, I could hit a good target about once in five times in practice and once in ten times in earnest. But the main reason that anybody could tell was that I didn't *wear* two guns, and never had, and never would. Because one was all that I wanted to have to manage.

Maybe you would think that a bright, sharp-eyed boy like that young Jigger Bunts would have seen a thing like that right off. And if it had been anybody else, he *would* have seen it. But where I stepped into the picture, there was no use. He was blind. He was blind on purpose. And he had been blind ever since the day that he had heard Sam Mitchell first tell those whopping lies about me.

Poor Jigger! He could have looked at me right in the middle of the day, and if I said that a spade was white, he would have sworn that I was right and he would have fought with anybody that hinted that maybe I might be wrong under some conditions. Jigger had found a hero, and he made that hero, with the help of those lying cowpunchers, fit in with everything that he could expect a hero to be.

I was faultless. I *had* to be faultless, because otherwise there wouldn't have been any thrill in me from Jigger Bunts's point of view.

I suppose by this time that you're beginning to see just what sort of a queer one he was. And yet not so queer, either, but just young. And anybody that's a man and young is bound to be sort of crazy in one direction or another.

He was satisfied with what he heard about nobody daring to make a joke on a two-gun man, and the blithering idiot grinned and looked happy, as though somebody had paid *him* a compliment.

Then all the boys swallowed hard and somebody remembered that sailor Charlie had been about to tell a whopper when he was interrupted by the poor victim—I mean me!

That fellow said: "Charlie, what was that fight that you was going to tell us about that the chief had in Boston?"

"Oh, yes," said Charlie. "But I guess that all you boys have read all about that fight in the papers. They was full of it at that time."

"I recollect reading about it," said Dago Pete, very serious. "But I never before had the luck to bump into anybody that was right there at the ringside."

And somebody else put in: "You'd think that old Tom, there, would loosen up once in a while and tell us a little something about himself. Wouldn't you, kid?"

Jigger looked over at me with a silly smile, as much as to say that it was just my modesty. And at that, everybody had a choking fit again.

"I recollect the gent that fought him was an English heavyweight named Jimmy Carson. You remember?"

"Sure, we remember," said those bland liars, and they looked the sailor right in the eye and nodded. And he went right along, confound him!

"This Carson was going to cut up a great name for himself on our side of the water. He had licked about everything that they had in old England. And when there was nobody else worthwhile over there for him to beat up, he landed in the U.S.A. Well, it happened along about that time that our partner, here, old Tom Reynard, he was out of a job and broke. And when he seen the papers about this Englishman landing in Boston, he up and went to a fight promoter and said he wanted to try his hand at licking Carson. And he showed what he could do in the fight line by knocking out two of the fighters that was in the training quarters. Or was it three that you knocked out that afternoon, Tom?"

It was against our unwritten law for any of those blackguards to appeal to me like that in the midst of their lying. I was about to rip into Charlie, but he saw danger in my eye and he went along, quick and easy.

"Anyway, he got the job. And I paid good money for a seat near the ring and I seen Tom and the Englishman come into the ring to put on their bout.

"The Englishman, he had an advantage of about thirty pounds in weight. He came in at two hundred and ten and Tom only stacked up at a hundred and eighty."

That was plain silly, of course. There was never a time in my life when I stripped at more than a hundred and fifty. And all those boys knew it, and the kid should have known it as well as anybody else.

But he never thought of doing any criticizing, of course. He just sat there with a fool grin on his face admiring me and whispering: "I never would think you weighed that much. You must be terrible solid, Tom."

"But what Tom lacked in weight," Charlie continued, "you'd better believe that he made up in muscle. He looked like Hercules . . . that was about all that he looked like, and you can believe me when I say it. He was just plain strong. It was sticking out all over him. And though he ain't quite the man that he was then, I guess most of you boys have seen Tom stripped and know what I mean."

Of course they knew what he meant—all of them except the kid. They knew that I had skinny arms and a sort of caved-in chest—from the time when a horse fell on me—and the kid must have seen me stripped along with the rest of them. But that didn't make any difference to him.

Every eye was fixed on him, sort of in fear, because it looked like Charlie was laying it on a lot too thick and that the kid would sure break in and ask some dangerous questions.

But not the kid. He just lay back and nodded his head and looked over and worshipped me some more.

And he says: "Yes, I would hate to have the chief lay hold of me in earnest."

Him with six foot of leathery muscle and iron bone to talk about and me with—all that God gave me, which wasn't very much. The boys looked at each other and choked again, and some of them got pretty red in the face. It was too much even for that devil, Charlie, he had to cut the story short.

"Well," he said, "of course you all know how it turned out. In the first round, the chief hit the beefeater in the ribs and after that John Bull skipped around and did a lot of fancy boxing for seven or eight rounds. But along in the ninth, I think it was, the chief thought that the crowd had had about enough for their money, and he stepped in and popped John Bull right on the mug.

"It was a terrible sight to see what happened. He busted Jimmy Carson's jaw in three places and Jimmy lay there on the floor of the ring, gagging and gasping . . . because outside of his jaw being broke, he had a set of false teeth knocked down his throat."

Chapter Six

That remark about the false teeth gave the boys the chance that they had to have, or otherwise they would have laughed themselves to death, I suppose. They lay back and yelled and shouted and beat each other on the back and cried for joy. And they looked at me and they looked at the kid, and they went into convulsions again until it was sort of dangerous to let it go on anymore.

And all the time what was the kid doing? Was he looking at them and seeing that there wasn't enough in that fool remark about the false teeth to have caused all of this laughter? No, sir, that is exactly what he was not doing. Like a miserable half-wit, he was looking at me and shaking his head and smiling at me and wondering that God had ever made any men as big and as strong and as dangerous and as all-around perfect as I was.

Until I wanted to take him by his thick neck and choke him to death. And when the others looked at him and saw that fool expression on his face, they just about died, it pleased them so much. But you can understand why I didn't laugh much. No, I could have killed them all, before I was really cooled off good.

Well, after a time they were able to pull

themselves together. And right away the kid says to Charlie: "And what happened then?"

"What happened then? Oh, nothing," says Charlie, "except that we in the crowd got old Tom up on our shoulders and carried him around Boston's streets until we come to the mayor's house and there we stayed and hollered and cheered and finally the mayor came out and made us a speech and invited Tom to come into the house and shake hands with him, and then Tom made a speech . . ."

"What did you say, Tom?" busted in the kid.

"I forget," I said, and I gave Charlie a wall-eyed look that promised him a beating the next time that I got him alone.

"It was a pretty slick speech," said Charlie. "One of the best that I ever heard, especial the part that was about Bunker Hill. That part was as good as out of a book."

Once more they gave a look at the kid to see whether he had swallowed this.

Yes, sir! Impossible as it might seem to you, confound me if he didn't sit right there and swallow the whole yarn without so much as saying: "How queer!" Oh, at eighteen he was a jim-dandy! I never at any other time in my life ever wanted to be an Indian. But if I could have been a chief with a band on the warpath, just then, I would have scalped the whole lot of them, but I would have turned the kid over to the women for torture—for being such a number-ten-sized fool!

No, all he did was to say: "I guess that stopped the John Bull from fighting for a while."

"Why, I suppose that you never had a fight with a man that could even warm you up, did you, chief?" says Charlie to me.

It was breaking the rule. As I said before, it was breaking the unwritten law that we had established, that no matter how they lied, they were not to ask me to back up what they said about me. But here was Charlie, as I've told you, breaking the rule right and left and asking me one question after another. And that was why— though I'll regret it right up to my dying day— that I turned loose and gave Charlie and the crowd the same coin that they had been paying out to me—lie for lie!

I said: "Yes, I was warmed up enough once!"

The boys saw that I meant trouble, and sailor Charlie broke right in with a sea story to shut me off. He said: "Speaking of being warmed up reminds me of a time that I was sailing in the *Flying Mist*, from New York to San Francisco, around the Horn . . ."

"Hey, Charlie!" broke in the kid.

Charlie tried to go right on talking, but the kid got red and stood up and walked across the room and put his big hand on the shoulder of Charlie.

And Charlie looked up to him and said: "What's the matter?"

"Maybe you didn't hear who was speaking when you interrupted him," said the kid.

"Well, who?" says Charlie.

"*He* was speaking," said Jigger Bunts. "The *boss* was speaking."

Just as he might have said: "You've barely missed thunder and lightning."

Well, to talk like that to any cowpuncher was talking pretty big and dangerous and it was hard medicine for any man to take. And Charlie was a tough one, you can be sure. So he looked Jigger up and down from the mizzenmast to the foremast, and backward again. And he saw those big boots—red-leather boots, the same as Tom Reynard's, of course. And he saw the old blue jeans, the same as mine. And the corduroy shirt, the same as my shirt was. And he saw, too, the bandanna that Jigger wore—with the knot that tied it, copied exact after mine. But most of all, he saw the man inside of those clothes, and as I've mentioned before, it was a very considerable man!

It was too much man for Charlie, and he swallowed and said: "I didn't hear that Tom was talking. Go ahead, Tom, if you remember."

There was something impudent about his way of saying that that made the kid hesitate and frown down at Charlie, as though he wasn't quite sure, but really thought that he ought to take a second off and tie Charlie into a bowline—a running bowline knot, at that!

But he finally seemed to decide that he would let Charlie live. And the kid went back to his corner and he sat down there and kept a dark eye on Charlie for a while.

The stage was cleared for me, and I prepared to knock about half the spots off of poor Jigger's hero—meaning myself.

"Yes," I said, "there was at least one time when I was warmed up, as you were saying. There was one time when I was licked fair and square by a better man than I ever dreamed of being."

The faces of the boys dropped in chunks about a mile long. They saw that their winter's sport seemed about to be done for.

But their long faces were nothing compared with the face of Jigger. He fair turned white, and he looked at me with his eyes staring out of his head.

"Licked?" he said. "Licked? Fair and square, did I hear you say?"

"Fair and square," I averred.

There was a minute of terrible silence. The kid was blinking at me and it was easy to see that he was a sick boy. The wrecks of what he had thought me to be were toppling around his mental ears, you might say.

"It was a fellow smaller than I am, too," I said.

That was putting the crown on the horror for poor Jigger. I could see the boys in the background behind Jigger shaking their heads at me like mad and holding up their hands in dumb prayer for me to stop and not go any further in ruining their indoor sport. But I wouldn't stop. It gave me a mighty lot of pleasure to sit there and torture *them* a little.

"Do you mind," Jigger said "waiting for a minute? I'd like to . . . to hear about that . . . but . . . I'll be back in a minute."

He got up and stumbled out of the bunkhouse. I suppose that he was needing the fresh air pretty bad. And the minute that he disappeared, those cowpunchers came swarming around me and begged me to turn the thing into a joke. They begged me pretty near with tears in their eyes not to have myself beaten up by somebody imaginary. But I just shook my head and told them that the game had gone far enough and that now I was going to step out of the picture and let somebody else be the hero.

They were mighty down-hearted, and Pete busted in.

"All right. If you're gonna step out of the picture, only give *us* a chance to make up a hero out of the gent that beat you up. Ain't that reasonable, Tom? Is that any more than reasonable . . . to make us a new hero for the kid?"

"Who shall it be?" I asked, weakening a little.

"Anybody," said Pete. "Anybody will do better than nothing. Anybody will fit in fine. Anybody you say."

"Give me a name for the gent that licked me so bad," I said.

There were a lot of pictures pasted against the inside walls of that bunkhouse. There were mostly pictures of pretty girls and actresses that had been clipped out of newspapers and magazines, and things like that. Pretty girls in wedding veils, and all that sort of thing. Because you've got no idea how sentimental a lot of horny-handed working men can be.

One of those pictures had been tacked up and it had blown down and was fluttering around on the floor with a big wet heel mark on it. And Pete, being sort of desperate, scooped that picture up and held it in his hand. And the underside of it was what he saw.

"Here," he said. "Here's a name that will do as good as anything, I suppose. Louis Dalfieri. How does that sound to you?"

"It sounds rotten!" says somebody.

But just then, back comes the kid.

He looked white and he looked sick. And he had a stately way about him, such as folks have when they've been through a tragedy. He walks in and he sits down and he drops his head and he stares at the floor.

I know that if you had handed him a letter saying that all his family had just been murdered, he wouldn't have looked half as sad as he did just then. And finally he said: "It doesn't seem possible! I can't believe it, Tom. I . . . I almost think that you were joking!"

"About Dalfieri?" I ask.

"Dalfieri?" he said, sharp and quick.

I had a sort of falling of the heart, because I suspected that that was a name that he might have heard. Because that was a big magazine photograph, and a picture of that size would hardly be given to anybody except a pretty important person—a statesman or an actor or a murderer, or some such sort of a thing.

And I couldn't see any caption under the picture. There was only the name and the rest of the paper had been clipped away.

But the kid said: "Dalfieri! That's a sort of a weak, foreign-sounding name. It sounds more impossible than ever that you should have been . . . defeated . . . by a man with a name like that."

Poor Jigger! He couldn't say licked. It didn't have enough dignity. He had to talk about beating as though it were the fall of an empire.

Chapter Seven

I saw that the coast was clear for the making of my lie. I just handed that picture across to the kid.

"Maybe you wonder why I would keep a picture like this hanging around on the wall," I said. "But read the name underneath it and you may be helped to understand."

He gave the picture one look, and then he laughed in a sick fashion.

"Is this the fellow who beat you?" he asked.

"Doesn't he look like much to you?" I said. "Well, he didn't look like much to me, either . . . not at first."

It was a shame to do it. And mind you, I would not have done it if I had been able to guess then what was going to happen later on. But that would have been asking too much. You can't expect a man to be a mind-reader.

The kid seemed more serious, then, and he took another long squint at that picture.

It was a pretty sad-looking sort of a man, between you and me. I've never seen one that I liked much less. This Dalfieri had one of those thin, dark-looking French-Italian sort of faces, with hollow cheeks, and little mean-looking eyes set close together, and a superior smile on his thin lips, and a little short mustache with the ends just pointed out a bit and rolled down sharp as needles with wax. No wonder the kid was pretty sick when he looked over that face. So was I. But you see, that was to be the point of the new joke—to take a silly-looking imitation man like that and make a hero out of him right from the start for young Jigger Bunts.

"I don't know," said Jigger, "but he doesn't seem like a very great fighting man, to me. How come this Dalfieri wears a big necktie like this?"

The fellow in the photograph maybe was an artist or wanted to be one. He wore long hair— very long, so that it came curling and swooping down and around his neck and his ears very grand. And he matched that hair off with a big black necktie that must have had about a yard and a half of silk in it. It fair flowed all over his chest. I never seen such a tie.

"Partner," said the kid to me, "you mean to say that anybody ever wore a tie like that out on the range?"

"Do I mean to say it?" I said. "I do. Why, yes, I suppose that all the boys saw Dalfieri wearing that necktie."

The kid looked around the circle, and they all nodded, perfectly grave. They had a fine talent for keeping their faces straight, that gang of crooks and thugs did! Nary a one of them so much as winked an eye, but they all stared straight back at him. Oh, they were a great lot.

"Without being laughed at?" the kid pursued.

"Without being laughed at," I said.

"Laughed at?" broke in Pete. "Laugh at Dalfieri? Why, kid, *nobody* was ever fool enough to laugh at Dalfieri after he made a name for himself."

"Where was that?" the kid asked.

You could see that he had forgot to be critical right away. As soon as he began to ask questions, he was a goner, and anybody could pull the wool right over his eyes.

"Down in Tucson," said Dago Pete. "I was down there, then. Dalfieri come into town looking just the way he does in that picture. Sort of weak and effeminate, he was to look at him. And when he come into the saloon where some of us boys was standing, we had to laugh. I never seen such a joke as that fellow was!

"He looked us over, standing there nice and easy with one elbow on the bar, and while he put his drink down, he was marking us, one by one. Very calm and savvy, for a gent in clothes like those!

"Pretty soon he says . . . 'Bartender, your place is rather crowded.'

" 'That's the way that I like to have it,' the bartender says.

" 'What you want is interesting, but not important,' says Dalfieri. 'Kindly ask some of them to step outside.'

"Coming from a fellow like that, it was staggering of course. That was the reason that nobody stepped right up and hit him. But before anybody got that idea into their heads, a pair of guns jumped from nowhere into the hands of that Dalfieri. I don't know where he was keeping them, and I still don't know how he got them out. But the important thing was that one minute there was no gun to be seen any place on him, and the next minute there were a pair of big Colts in his hands, and he was waving the muzzles of them slow and easy over the whole crowd of us. I remember that he had one heel cocked up on the bar rail. And the corner of his eye was glued down on the bartender, over to the side and behind him. But still he seemed to have plenty of eyes for the rest of us.

" 'You heard me talk,' he said. 'I said that I wanted air. And now, get out of here and let a gentleman drink in peace.' "

Here Pete eased up and took a breath, which you'll agree that a man would need after telling offhand a lie of the size of that one. And we all sat around pretty still, waiting to see if the kid would swallow it.

Well, he was so easy that there was hardly any fun in it. He was simply petrified, he was so amazed and so interested. And he could barely whisper: "Well, did you all walk out?"

"Young fellow, we did," said Pete very quiet. "We walked right outside of that saloon!"

"Wonderful!" the kid said, with his black eyes burning and blazing. "It doesn't seem possible."

"We stood around outside of that saloon for a while," Pete continued, "and pretended that the only reason that we had walked out in the first place was because we wanted to figure out what would be bad enough to do to a fellow that had the nerve to step in and talk like that to a bunch of real bad actors like we were. But speaking personal, I have to admit that I knew from the start that *I* didn't want any part of his game. He had that nice, quiet, cold look in the eye that means nasty work when you got him cornered. I didn't want to do any of the cornering. And most of the other boys must have figured him the same way, because after he had finished his drink very deliberate, standing up there and chattering away with the bartender, he turned around and come sashaying out of that saloon and walked through what was left of the crowd.

"Most of the boys had sneaked away. But still, there must have been seven or eight left. And not a one lifted a hand, and not a word was said, and nobody so much as met his eye. I was there and I know.

"But that same night some greasers from over

the river met up with our friend Dalfieri and got a foolish idea about running him around a little, because in their part of the country they were looked up to a whole lot for being real bold bad actors. All that Dalfieri done was to kill two of 'em and wounded another so bad that he had to have his arm cut off . . . and two more was not shot up so bad, but that they could ride out of town. Which they done and never bothered anybody in Tucson again.

"But after we heard about that, we didn't feel so bashful about the way we had let that fellow walk over us. We just felt that we had used mighty good sense, y'understand?"

The kid was simply paralyzed.

"Five men!" he kept saying over and over again. "Think of standing up to five white men all at the same time . . . and beating them all!"

He sat there letting that grand idea soak in.

"What become of Dalfieri?" he asked at last. "But still . . . did he really beat you, Tom?"

You could see that Pete had warmed up the youngster to the point where it was *possible* for him to believe that somebody might have beaten me. But still, it was bitter medicine.

I decided to bury myself six feet under the ground, so far as being a fighter in the estimation of young Jigger Bunts was concerned.

I said: "I had sense enough not to step out with guns, when Dalfieri was around. He and I had it out with fists, and what he did to me was enough till I hollered quits . . ."

Jigger Bunts jumped up out of his chair. His voice was full of agony. Real pain.

"You don't mean that you asked him to stop?"

"Don't I?" I said. "But I do, though, and if you had been there, you would have done the same thing. It was like trying to tag a lightning bolt, or wrestling with a panther."

The kid sat down very slowly. And all the time he was staring at me, and all of the time I could feel myself sinking millions of miles out of the place where Jigger's stars was kept and down past the moon, even, and right down to the earth, where he shrugged his shoulders and gave his eyes a rub and looked at me, and saw me for the first time—saw my caved-in chest and my skinny neck, and—the fact that I carried only one gun. In fact, saw that I was just a common or garden variety of cowpuncher such as you could pick up a hundred of in any little range town.

You might think that it would have grieved me some to lose out in his respect so far. No, it didn't. I was tired of wearing wings and claws and epaulettes, and such stuff. And I wanted to appear just as myself. I had been through too much grilling to enjoy being famous—in the eyes of one man.

"I don't think," says Jigger Bunts after a while, and in a very soft voice, "I don't think . . . that all the hell that there is could make me give up. I don't think that I could holler quits."

He shivered. The idea seemed to make him sick. Because he was just eighteen, and at eighteen a man is prouder than a lion and an eagle rolled into one.

And then—well, he turned his shoulder toward me a little and he started asking Pete some more about Dalfieri.

And Pete had had a chance to think up a lot of new things.

In another minute, Pete was telling the kid how Dalfieri could work two six-guns from the hip.

And there sat the kid, shaking his head and smiling and wondering and enjoying this new hero, just as much as he had ever enjoyed me.

The boys picked up heart again. Because they saw that though I had stepped myself out of trouble, I had put in a substitute who was almost as good fun. They didn't have the pleasure of laughing at the kid and at me, but they made up for that by concentrating all the harder on Jigger Bunts.

Chapter Eight

This Dalfieri began to get more terrible than you can imagine, right away. There was still the biggest part of the winter to work away on the kid, and the boys fair spread themselves to do a good job. The first thing you know, they had turned Dalfieri into an outlaw, because they got him into so many shooting scrapes and had him killing so many men that they had to make him an outlaw.

But that was all the better. After he became an outlaw, he began to hold up stages and rob banks and raise hell generally for the benefit of that poor loon of an eighteen-year-old boy and the rest of us in the bunkhouse.

The reason that I take so much of the blame is because I began to guess that serious consequences were coming long before the truth was known. I began to guess that this would not be such a pretty story when we got all through.

It was not so bad at first. By degrees we could see the kid turning himself into Dalfieri. The way it began was that one day Pete noticed that the kid had not shaved his upper lip. He whispered the news around, but none of us would believe it. But the day after, there was no doubt at all. There was a fine black shadow on the kid's upper lip.

It grew very fast. He was always combing it and brushing it and taking fine care of it, and almost before you knew it, there he was with a short little black mustache, as close to the mustache in the picture as you could imagine.

That was rich cream for the cowpunchers, of course. I suppose that no mustache from the beginning of the world ever made so many grown men happy as that one did.

How could a proud and sensitive youngster act like that? I *don't* know. Unless it's true that men really are a little crazy when they're young—which it is my conviction that they are. But there was the mustache for us to look at, as big as day. And that was not all. Nor hardly the half.

He began to take a lot of care of his hair, we noticed. Week by week, it grew longer and longer. And there was a natural wave in it which he had been ashamed of before, and which he was always trying to sleek out of his hair. He stopped sleeking it, now. He let those waves begin again and he gave them a lot of encouragement, and pretty soon when he was galloping along in the snow, there was a little flutter of hair behind the nape of his neck.

He took a lot of care of himself in other ways, too.

He had two pairs of boots. One pair of cowhide he used to wear to work. The other pair he kept in the bunkhouse and he took mighty good care of them. Every day he gave them an extra coat of polish and he rubbed them and suppled them up. Can you imagine that young fool coming back from the range and shining himself all up for a *bunkhouse?* That was exactly what he did!

I don't think that he was exactly conscious of what he was doing. And if you had asked him if he was trying to make himself look like Dalfieri, he would have said that he wasn't, but that he had just taken a sudden interest in well-polished boots and in long hair with a curl in it.

But the crowning stroke is something that I can hardly believe even after seeing it and which I hate to write down here, because it may make everything seem untrue.

However, the fact is that he got hold of an old black silk shirt that one of the boys had. It was worn out and so he got it cheap. Then we saw him working at that shirt every day. And pretty soon he had made a long strip of silk, bound up with thread on each side. And the next night after that, at the same time that he put on his shined up boots, he got out that black silk and he spent a long time over himself, so that he was late for dinner. And when he did come in, I had to bury my face behind my big tin coffee cup, even though I scalded myself very bad and some of the coffee went down the wrong way, so that I began to cough and sputter. But I noticed that a lot of the other boys were the same way, and there was one—I think that it was that sailor, Charlie—who swallowed half of a hot boiled potato and went hopping around the floor on one foot, holding his stomach with both hands and hollering that he was burned to death inside.

By this you can judge that there was a lot of commotion, but there was a pretty good cause for it, because there was our kid as big as life, with his short mustache all waxed out with candle grease at the ends, and with his long hair all brushed back and curling past his ears, and with a great big black silk necktie, done into a big flowing bowknot!

Even now, at this distance, even though I have thought about it a lot of times since, I can hardly persuade myself that anybody could be foolish enough to do such a thing in such a place. But there he was—really a sight for sore eyes.

After a while we were able to go on with supper, but all the way through the meal, somebody would begin sputtering. And Pete just had to get up and leave the table. And then, outside, we could hear a sound that was like the baying of a wolf—except that it was Pete's way of laughing.

I muttered something about Pete maybe being sick and going out to look after him, and I went outside, and Pete and I braced up against each other, and held each other up as we laughed and cried and laughed again.

After a while, we came in and the kid asked

me very sad and serious and quick if I had been sick—my face was so red and swollen up and my eyes was so full of tears. You see, the kid had not entirely dropped me. I wasn't a real hero to him anymore, but still he felt very friendly toward me. I had meant so much to him once that I couldn't be shut out of the picture, as they say, altogether.

That was a wild evening!

But the necktie was not the worst of it. It was not more than the beginning, in a manner of looking at it.

Because, a little while before that, we had noticed that the kid was now spending a lot of his time off by himself. And then, one day, one of the boys, riding up behind a hilltop, saw the kid pacing on the other side with two revolvers strapped onto his saddle. And every minute he was snatching out those two guns, one in each hand, and snapping them, hip-high.

Shooting from the hip, you see, after the style of the great Dalfieri.

Of course that made a pretty good story when it was told in the bunkhouse the same evening, and I didn't pay much attention to it at the time, except to laugh, just as everybody else was laughing. But a little while later, as I was saying, I got my first hint of what was coming.

We had a bright, rather warm day—for February! And in the middle of the afternoon we heard a couple of shots behind the barn. A little while later one the boys, named Chuck Narvin, a Canadian, came running into the bunkhouse, looking pretty queer.

He said that he had been in the barn, cleaning out, and that he had looked outside and seen the kid come up and begin to go through a whole lot of antics, snatching out his guns, and aiming them from the hip at a couple of tin cans that he stuck up on two posts a good distance away.

And then both of those guns went off—*Bang! Bang!*—and he looked out, laughing to himself—and what he saw was one of the cans standing on the post the same as before. *But one of those cans was on the ground!*

You had better believe that it took the wind out of our sails when we heard that.

Of course, there is a lot of talk about two-gun men, but mostly it is just plain nonsense. And, really, I don't think that what they call a two-gun man in the storybooks ever existed. That is to say, a man who could take aim with two guns at the same time and hit two different targets in the same pull of the triggers. However, I may be wrong, because now and then you'll see some very fancy trick shooting done. I only mean to say that in all my days I've seen quite a few who packed two guns, but that was only because it gave them *twelve* shots instead of six—but they did all their shooting with one hand.

That is to say, all except maybe three or four. Now and then you would run into a fellow who was naturally ambidextrous, and that fellow could handle two guns, but the way that he did it was just to fire off one gun and then the other— hip-high or breast-high, I don't care which. That way, they could keep up a pretty quick stream of lead flying. Though for my part, I think that they might have done just as well or better if they had left the second gun in the holster and concentrated on shooting straight with just one kicker at a time. It is all well to throw a lot of lead into the air, but one bullet in the right spot is just as satisfactory as a thousand spread out over the corners of a target.

However, what I am driving at is that it was a mighty rare thing to see a two-gun man make his Colts talk together. And here was this kid, Jigger Bunts, right among us, who was able to do that thing! You can bet that we began to look with a different sort of an eye at him.

It wasn't accident, his hitting that can, either.

I think it was only two or three days after that that I myself saw him blaze away at a couple of stones that he had put up on a bank. And that time he got *both* of the stones—one right after the other, shooting so quick that the explosions stumbled one on top of the other. Those were big stones, and at short range. And the kid was one of those naturally left-handed people who have been forced to learn to use their right from the time they are babies—so that he could think about as well with one hand as with the other.

So it wasn't so very wonderful, after all. However, there was enough to it to make me see the danger.

Chapter Nine

What it showed me was that Jigger was blazing away pounds and pounds of powder and lead trying to make his skill something like the skill of Dalfieri. But no matter how many hours a day he practiced, he never could come anywhere near to it. The reason was that we had Dalfieri doing things that the devil himself would have gaped at. Nothing was too much for Dalfieri, and poor Jigger was trying to model himself after a man that never was! However, when a bright boy like that started after a goal, he was apt to go a long distance toward it, and the farther off it was from him in the beginning, the greater distance he would go. He was beginning to look a little tragic, now, because he saw that he could never be a regular story-book dead-shot Dick, like Dalfieri. But still he set his teeth and kept plugging.

And I got the boys together one day and said to them: "What if this kid should one day cut loose and start smearing somebody up . . . according to the pattern that this here Dalfieri of ours has been using?"

It was old Tod Minter of Chicago who spoke up and said: "There's no danger of that. The kid is too damned good-natured and kind to ever do anybody any harm."

I am glad that I can write down that I gave that warning. It takes some of the load off of my shoulders. And I remember that we all talked it over, beginning to end, and the boys all swore that there would never be any harm done because Jigger was just a kid who was playing a game of suppose right out loud, as you might say. But they all swore that he would never let it go too far. And they said that it was a good thing for him to be making a damned fool of himself out there where we all knew him and liked him and where nobody had any malice against him.

I thought that they were right. I thought that there was just that much idiocy that Jigger Bunts had to get out of his system, and so I let them go right on with their one-ring circus through the rest of the winter.

Not all the way through the winter, though, because it was early in April that the bust came.

It had been a pretty hard winter. And now the cows were getting thin and pretty down at the head and the snow was packed and jammed down so that the poor devils could hardly paw it away from the bunchgrass that was lying underneath. Take a general look around, and you would say that this was the real heart of winter—January, say. But it was April and the big thaw couldn't be very many days off.

It was just at that time that Jigger Bunts came riding up to the bunkhouse with a stranger along by his side.

Now I wish to God that I never saw that man!

He was one of those lank, yellow-skinned, greasy-looking sort of handsome fellows. Dirty-looking and handsome. And he had a smile that the ladies might have liked, but which I didn't. He looked smart. And if there is anything in the world that I hate, it's a smart fellow.

We were all gathering around the kitchen and getting ready for supper when the pair of them came riding up. I remember remarking that it was kind of funny to be eating supper by daylight, after taking our chuck by smoky lantern light for so many months. And Minter of Chicago laughs and says that it all depends on the kind of chuck, whether it's better to see it by daylight or by lamplight. Which he thought that in this camp, lamps might be good enough.

Not very much of a joke, but it doesn't take much of a joke to get a laugh out of a cow outfit that has a whole long winter behind it. On top of this, somebody came in and let the kitchen screen door bang behind him.

"Here's the kid coming along and he's picked up a stranger," says the fellow that came in. To this day, I can't recollect his name. And he says:

"I hope to God that he ain't spilled all that he knows about Dalfieri to this new gent and got himself waked up to the facts!"

We all tried to jam ourselves into the doorway, wanting to see who was coming, but not wanting to get out too far into the cold wind that was tearing over the snow.

I remember saying that by the way the pair of them were pounding along, they were riding for something more than supper. They came smashing up to the door and tumbled out of their saddles and I took a good long look at this stranger and, as I said before, didn't like anything that I saw.

He said: "Are these the fellows that have been giving you that guff?" And he laughed a little.

"These," said the kid, as stiff as a poker, "are the men who have told me. They will tell you, too."

Jigger walked the stranger into the kitchen. He said: "Partners, I want you to meet a gentleman that I picked up today while I was riding herd. This is Bud Crandall. Crandall, I want you to meet . . ."

And he went the whole circle of us, beginning with the cook, and doing it in a sort of proud, deferential way that he had, to show how proud he was that he knew men like us. Oh, the kid could make you feel like a king with that manner of his! And he wound up with me, and he stepped

69

back and said: "And I suppose that even if you have not heard of Louis Dalfieri, you have at least heard of Tom Reynard."

"I'm glad to know you, Reynard," says the stranger, "but I got to admit to this kid, here, that I'm damned if I ever heard of you before. But I hope that you ain't in a class with the sort of history that Bunts here has been filling me full on."

I could see the kid just reach for the shoulder of Pete and squeeze it, to sort of steady himself, and by the look on Pete's face I knew that every one of those five fingers must have gone clear to the bone. Oh, the kid had a grip and a half, I can tell you.

But when he had cleared some of his heat out of himself, he was able to say, very stiffly: "I told this gentleman, while we were riding along, that story that you were telling last week, Tom, about how Dalfieri shot the three sparrows for the three thousand dollars. And Mister Crandall seemed disposed to doubt the story and he wished to meet the men who had told it to me. And so, Mister Crandall, I have had the pleasure of bringing you here."

The more politer the kid got, you could lay to it to the madder he was. And now he was boiling for certain. But this Bud Crandall was cool. He had plenty of nerve. I have to say that for him. He just looked us over and shrugged his shoulders.

70

"It can't be done," he said. "Not with a revolver. And I doubt it with a rifle, even. I doubt it a lot!"

"It was a Colt, Tom, was it not?" confirmed the kid.

I was in a sweat, I had almost forgotten that idiot story that I had told the week before about how Dalfieri the Great had made a bet with somebody that he could shoot a sparrow in a cluster that was across the road from him. And the man bets Dalfieri that he would give him a thousand dollars for every sparrow he hit, and Dalfieri was to pay five hundred for every shot that didn't bring down something. So out with his Colt, the great Dalfieri whacks off the head of one sparrow while they're perched across the road on the fence, and then as they flutter away in a cloud, he smashes two more of them all to smithereens, and not much more than two puffs of feathers come floating down to earth. I had told the story, all right, and it was considered such a mild lie to tell about our Dalfieri that the boys would hardly listen to me as I finished it off. Well, I had told the story and here were the big, bright black eyes of the kid fixed on me.

"I suppose it was a revolver, all right," I said, pretty unhappy.

Of course Crandall could see that I was lying, and he started in to ride me for it. Yes, he had plenty of nerve. He didn't care whether he was in a strange camp or not. He didn't take anything from anybody.

He started to say: "Well, Reymond . . ."

"Rey*nard* is the name," Jigger said, very nasty. "I wish that you could remember . . ."

That tone would never do for a minute, and I stepped in and said: "Jigger, Crandall is our guest and I guess that you've almost forgotten it. I think that you'd better take the horses and put them up."

That was a good deal to say to a man-eating, young ripper with an ambidextrous pair of Colts wandering around himself.

But the kid looked on me as a sort of mixture of elder brother and uncle, you might say. All he did was to give me a sad, reproachful look, and then he turned around on his heel and took the horses away.

As soon as he was gone, we all got to work and explained things to Crandall. And he understood right away. He laughed until the tears came and then he let up, and then he laughed some more. He said that he wouldn't give us away, and he didn't. But the way he acted was all the worse. He sneered at the kid all the way through supper, and I could see Jigger getting more and more hot and more and more restless.

The way that Jigger had when he was mad was to lift up his head a little higher, then look you right in the face with his eyes extra wide open, as if he were saying: "You seem to be a stranger to me. What are you doing in *this* house?"

He gave this Crandall a few looks like that, but Crandall just laughed in his face. And I could see the nostrils of the kid quiver.

I knew right then, as I sat across the table from him and stared at his face, that this kid was apt to be a dangerous customer someday. And the day was perhaps not so far off. And while I sat there watching him, I decided that we had been playing with a young bear cub and not with any house dog at all.

So I made up my mind that I would call the pack off this young bear before he put his teeth in somebody and spoiled them for life.

Those were good resolutions. The only trouble with them being that they were just too late. One day sooner, and everything might have been saved. But as a matter of fact, the danger itself was right on top of me before my eyes were opened to it.

Chapter Ten

Right after supper, the kid got up and lined away for the bunkhouse, instead of sitting around the table the way we always did at night, telling stories—and most of the stories about Dalfieri, of course. Pete loosened up with a yarn right after supper, but the kid wouldn't even stay to hear it halfway through. He got up and stalked out of the room.

"The kid don't like me," Crandall observed. And he laughed in a damned mean way.

"Stranger," I said to him, "I want you to be comfortable here and I hope you get along all right with everybody. But I've got this to say that may sort of put you on the right track. We've had a lot of fun with the kid, but we all like him a lot. I guess that I can speak up for myself and say that I like him about as well as any man that I ever sat across the table from in my whole life!"

That should have been enough to make him see what I meant, but it wasn't. There was something just mean in that Crandall. He *liked* trouble. He would go down a rabbit's hole to find trouble, if he couldn't get it any other way.

"Well," he said, "I guess that's *your* business. I can't say that he looks more than any other young fool, to me!"

A pretty nasty remark, but I let that remark slide, me being the boss and Crandall our guest. A man has to look over a whole lot when he is the host—particularly in the West. And so, right after supper, I started a little game of cards and got the stranger into it.

That was another bad lead on my part because I should have known by one look at the ratty eye of that Crandall and his long, thin, soft hands, that he was probably a cardsharper.

And he was, too. He turned the game into poker in about five minutes, and with their cash on the table before them, my men started trying to beat Crandall.

It was like a trout trying to catch a shark. He simply tied them in knots. I don't know how many crooked tricks there are in cards, but I'll guess that that rat used about nine-tenths of them before the evening was over. And all for about sixty-five dollars. That was not much, you'd say. But it was a good deal to a lot of cowpunchers, who worked for less than half of that a month.

When the game had gone that far, I saw that the rest of the money in camp was pretty sure to go the same way, and so I broke up the game and got a pretty hard look from Crandall on account of it.

He went to the bunkhouse with us and took the blanket and the bunk that we offered to him without thanking us.

When he was undressing, he produced a couple

of revolvers. One was shoved inside his trousers, and one was slung under the pit of his left arm. He showed them to us, pretty proud of the way he had them packed away.

"I've never shot sparrows like this . . . Dalfieri," Crandall said, "but I've shot things with less feathers on them." And he laughed in that mean way of his.

Of course that remark was aimed at the kid, and I could see Jigger twitch in his bunk as the shot went home, you know.

The next morning I made up my mind that I would see to it that the pair of them didn't spend too much time close together. So I herded the kid through an early breakfast and sent him off to do something—I don't remember what—that should have taken him a long distance from the house.

He knew why I was sending him, I suppose, and he was very glum about it.

He said in that dignified way of his: "Tom, I feel that I've been insulted by that Crandall."

I said: "Old-timer, now don't you be a damned fool. You run along and mind your own business. I tell you, he's a rat."

"All right," said the kid. "You wouldn't want me to do anything that wasn't honorable, I guess."

"Of course not," I told him, and away he sails for the barn. But he turns sharp around and comes back to me.

76

"I hear that he has taken a lot of money off of the boys while they was entertaining him," he says.

"Do you hear that?" I said. "You hear too much. You run along and don't bother me. The boys haven't lost anything they didn't deserve to lose, so far as you're concerned."

Which was nothing but the truth, of course.

But the kid went off, very thoughtful. However, I would not have dreamed that he would disobey me. He had always used my commands like gospel law. I had no real reason to suspect him.

After breakfast, Crandall hung around for a while and got the cook to put him up a snack, because it was such a long ride to town. Then he suggested another game of poker, but I told him that we had lost enough for one trip, and I saw him off and wished him luck.

Not that I really *wanted* to see him have good luck, but because I was just so glad to have that loafer off my hands and out of the camp before he and the kid got tangled and had to be cut apart with a pair of wire tweezers.

So I saw him ride away, with his two guns shoved away out of sight in his clothes, a plain bad actor if there ever was one. And then I went back into the kitchen to sit by the stove and figure up some accounts, because I had to do the clerking as well as the bossing, and a lot of hard riding and all the rest. Yes, the Bar L certainly made a man work for his extra fifteen dollars a week, and I'm here to state that fact.

It was slow work. I suppose that I was a couple of hours in there and when I got it all straightened out, I went out and saddled up a horse for myself and got ready to ride. I had the saddle on the horse when the fool—it was Roman-nosed, high-headed idiot—began to buck and didn't leave off until it had sucked the saddle off and trampled on the saddle, and had an all-around good time.

I stood by and let him work it out of his system, and at the same time I promised him that he would go on the kid's string the very next day. Because it seemed that he was full of the stuff the kid liked to practice on.

He eased off and I had the saddle on him the second time and everything cinched up, and just as I was about to work the bit between his teeth, the cook came running out to me and showed me a handful of gold pieces.

"Where the devil did you get those?" I asked him.

Because he had no right to have sixty or seventy dollars in his hands.

The cook was Chinese, you see, and he never could speak very good English at any time, and when he was excited, like this, he could hardly talk anything.

He said: "You frien', all-same lil' Jigger . . . he bling . . ."

Well, I can't write that lingo down, and the funny sound of all the words.

I said: "Wong, will you shut up and take a breath and try to talk straight, dammit."

I never did have any patience with the Chinese, I don't know why. But Wong was a particularly aggravating one, he talked with a lisp, among other things. Whoever heard of a Chinese man having a lisp wished into him.

The only man in camp who treated Wong decent was the kid, because the kid was decent to everybody and everything. Why, he couldn't even climb on a horse without patting him on the neck and calling him: "Good boy." And even when a horse had bucked him off and landed him on his head—which happens to everybody now and then when they're learning the ways of Indian ponies—the kid would get up and just grin. You never saw him taking out his bad temper on a horse. Same way with Wong. Everybody else used Wong to unlimber their tongues, because he didn't understand much of the way he was cussed, and because it didn't make much difference if he did. But the kid was different. I think I mentioned how he introduced Wong to that rat, Bud Crandall.

"Mister Wong, Mister Crandall." Like that.

But anyway, Wong loved the kid. I suppose we all loved the kid. But as the Frenchmen say, the way Wong loved him was something extra special. He would smile all over his ivory face every time he heard the name Jigger.

So he had to get himself untangled from a lot of wasted emotion before he could tell me the story, which was that the kid had come riding up to the door of the kitchen and told Wong that here was the money that the boys had lost to the gambler. He said good bye to Wong, and he wanted Wong to say good bye to all the boys from him, particularly to me. He had written out a little note for my benefit,

I grabbed the note from Wong and ripped it open. It said:

Dear Chief,

I am sorry that this has happened. Most of all, I'm sorry that I broke my word to you and went after him. But I couldn't help it. I got to thinking it over, and the more I thought about the way he had talked to you and the way he had sneered at everything that was said to him, the angrier I got. Finally I just had to light out after him. I had a little talk with him, and he was hurt. I am going to get him into town and, with a little doctoring, I think that he will live. Of course, I regret everything. Most of all, I regret having to go away so that I can no longer have your example to live up to and follow. Chief,

I have to tell you that you have been a grand man for me to know, and I think that remembering you will keep me from ever sinking too low!

Affectionately,
Jeremy Bunts

P.S. I suppose that it isn't necessary for me to tell you that I shall not submit to arrest. Of course, no man of honor could allow a sheriff to capture him. Good bye, Tom. Someday I'll see you again unless they hunt me down in the meantime.

I leaned on Wong waiting for my head to clear. The poor man was pretty sure that something was wrong with the kid, but he didn't know what. And he kept blubbering and wanting to know is: "Lil' Jigger plenty seek . . . no?"

Finally I got my wind, grabbed that Roman-nosed fool of a horse, and started burning the quirt into him while I headed for town.

Chapter Eleven

There was only one town that any sensible man would start for from the ranch, and that was Marion Crossing, down on the river. So I headed for that town, and I rode all that day cursing the stiff gait of the pony and wishing that snow would all be damned. I started about midmorning, and I got there about midnight. There was a good stiff wind out of the north and the snow was coming down just fast enough to be miserable, trickling down your neck and swirling in front of your eyes. And when I saw the lights of Marion Crossing they looked pretty comfortable to me and the poor pony was so dog-goned tired that he just stopped right there on top of the hill and stretched himself out and neighed to tell how mighty glad he was that there was an end to that trail.

But while that fool bronco was neighing his head off and while I sat there looking at the winking of the lights, something spoke up inside of me and told me that I would never get to the kid in time to head him off from doing something foolish.

You can't afford to overlook it when a voice like that talks up inside of you. There is generally something behind it. And as I looked at those lights I said to my horse: "It ain't any use. That town ain't big enough to hold the news that I want to find in it."

But I jogged along into Marion Crossing and had a walloping time getting the hotel owner out of bed and prying a place to sleep out of him. He was a sore-headed old German that always went around with one suspender on and one suspender off and a big flapping pair of slippers that turned away up at the toes.

I said, nice and polite, would he tell me if Jigger Bunts and Bud Crandall had hit that town that evening.

He only growled: "For vot am I? A newspaper, ain't it? Could I know yet all vot foolishness iss . . . ?"

I shut him up quick. I was too tired and too mad to be bothered listening to a lingo like that. I asked him could he talk American, and if he couldn't, I didn't want to hear any of his yap, and would he show me a room before I broke him in two and fed the pieces to the dogs. Finally I told him he should go out and see that my horse had all it could eat and a stall.

Well, I got to my room, but I couldn't even go to bed, I was so sick. I just sat there on the side of that bed and held my head in my hands and thought. I mean, I tried to think, but I couldn't.

Then I would say to myself: "The kid is well-raised . . . and he's got a good education under his belt . . . and he ain't going to step out and do anything that's too foolish."

But all the time I knew that I was lying to myself. I knew that he was eighteen years old. That's the answer. I knew that he had come to what you might call the time limit and something had to happen to him. He had gone all winter only talking foolish, and now he would cut and smash something. I just didn't know what.

But oh, how my hands had to get ahold of him. If I could only have gone to him or yelled to him, just to say: "Jigger, it ain't so bad as all this. You've just man-handled a dirty crook who *needed* man-handling, and nobody is going to want to arrest you."

Well, then I would say to myself that when he got into the other town—because now I knew that he had headed the wrong way and had gone all the way to New Nineveh.

I should think that even hearing that name a man would have better sense than to go to a town like New Nineveh. There was nothing new about it, in the first place, except the front half of its name. It was just an awful mistake, that town was.

But there was my Jigger Bunts, poor kid.

Then I told myself that I would have to answer up to the boys back at the ranch if I didn't find the kid.

I had just got that far in my thinking, when I heard somebody downstairs.

"Will you stop that walkin' around? The rest of us want to sleep!"

I forgot to say that I was not sitting on the side of the bed now. I was walking up and down. Because I couldn't stand it, sitting still. I would have busted. When I heard that fellow downstairs yap, I ran to the door and jerked it open and I yelled: "If you come here to this place to sleep, *I've* come here to walk. And by God, walk I shall. And if you don't like the style of my walking, why don't you come up here and show me another way of doing it."

That was foolish, yes. It was boyish, crazy. But just then if a man had come up to me with a cannon in each hand and said that he wanted to fight, I would have wept with joy. That was the way I was feeling, if you can understand what I mean.

And I went back into my room and began stamping up and down the floor. It was amazing how much better that made me feel.

That was Out West in the wild and wooly days and perhaps you wonder how it happened that I didn't have all the other roomers up there inquiring for the place where I wanted to be buried in the morning, after they had got through with me. But between you and me, the West as I found it was never so really bad and wild—except in spots.

And that night I was the bad and wild spot, and

all the suckers in that hotel knew it, too, you had better believe me. All I heard after a time were groans.

"Please, stranger, I'm a hard-working man. I'd like to sleep, real well, if you don't mind."

Of course, I eased up and walked soft for a while after that. But that hotel wasn't intended to have much peace that night. Because about an hour later, while I was swinging myself from side to side on the bed, and trying to think of something to do, somebody else began to bang on the front door. And the poor old German had to go flap-flapping down the stairs again, dropping language all the way down something remarkable to listen to. You take it generally, a foreigner can always cuss in two languages a long time before he can speak either of them by grammar.

There was not much talk wasted down there below. There was just a stampede up the stairs and my door was busted open and there stood Pete and Charlie the sailor glowering down at me, with hope fading out of their faces little by little.

"Hell!" said Charlie. "You're the gent that just come in from . . . oh, hell!"

Yes, they had heard the news a long time after I left, and they had made better time in than I had. Three more of the boys were coming along behind.

"Why didn't you bring Wong, too?" I yelled.

"He wanted awful bad to come," they said.

They didn't see that there was something of the nature of a joke in what I had said.

No, they were not seeking jokes and they were not making any jokes that night. You might say that they had used up all the laughs that were in their system.

They just lingered around, propping themselves against the wall and staring at each other very gloomy, too tired to stand up and too nervous to sit down.

When they said anything it was in a sort of robber's whisper, if you know what I mean.

"Well, chief, we thought that maybe numbers would come in handy. In case they had put him in the jail, you see."

I smiled on them. It did me a lot of good, I can tell you to smile down on them, very calm and superior.

"So that you could beat down the wall of the jail and fetch him out, I suppose," I said.

They didn't answer me. They didn't need to. Charlie got out an old Colt that should have been wearing white hair, and began to rub it up and oil it up, very affectionate and thoughtful.

"Oh, I don't know," Pete said in that same sort of a dying whisper. "We didn't know what we would have to do . . . I suppose he's gone on to New Nineveh?"

I said I supposed he had.

"It's too bad," said Charlie. "They're a mean bunch, over there. They hate their town so bad that they take it out on everybody that comes along."

And he didn't say *that* for a joke, either!

"But Jigger is only a fool," said Pete. "Even over there, they will see that he's a nice clean kid and no more, and they will not act like damned fools!"

Charlie answered: "Nobody but damned fools live in New Nineveh. Otherwise, why would they be there?"

They went on talking like that, nice and cheerful.

"Shoot a man," said Charlie, "and then take him into a town . . . and when you get into town, refuse to be arrested . . . because it ain't honorable . . ."

He couldn't say any more. Of course he had picked up my note where I dropped it in the corral. The boys had had a peek at it.

And Pete said: "But the kid is going to be all right. He's been raised pretty good by Tom Reynard. He has had fine examples held up to him of gentlemen conduct he has. Dalfieri, that low skunk! Things like Dalfieri has been held up to him. Gunfighters! Yes, that's how a poor kid like that has been raised. My God, Reynard, I should have thought that you would pretty near die, you would be that sick with yourself!"

Yes sir. You won't believe it, but I'm repeating pretty close to the exact words that he used on me. After raising hell with the kid and with me for most of the winter; after doing all the really effective lying about Dalfieri—it's *me* that they blamed.

I ask you!

Then Pete broke out: "Have you telegraphed?"

It went through me like light through a chunk of ice. No! I hadn't thought of doing that. They gave me one terrible look, and then we tore for the telegraph office. The operator was not there. We found him. He wanted to dress for the cold night, but we told him damn the cold night and we helped him down to the office and watched him unlimber his key and begin to make it tick.

Then after a while he said: "All right. I got them."

Pretty soon, he stopped ticking, having sent our message, and then he began to listen and write, and he read it out for us, what the ticker had said back. Which was plenty. It ran like this:

WE WANT BUNTS AS MUCH AS YOU DO BUT HE PASSED THROUGH TOO FAST FOR US TO CATCH HIM DO YOU KNOW HIS HOME ADDRESS

(Signed)

NEW NINEVEH

We looked for a long time at that telegram. But there was no way of reading any other meaning into it.

You will admit that a telegram is a pretty poor place for a joke. But the people in New Nineveh were just like that. As Charlie the sailor said: "What could you expect from a lot of bums that never had any bringing up."

Chapter Twelve

There were forty miles between New Nineveh and Marion Crossing. And while the boys were going back toward the hotel to talk things over, I decided that one man can work faster than three, especially when there are forty miles to be covered. So I got to the livery stable and showed them my tired horse and asked for a trade. I had dragged the owner out of bed at three in the morning, and so he wanted to charge me twenty dollars, but when I pointed out to him that although my pony had a Roman nose, it had a fine disposition and when he saw that the poor brute wouldn't kick when he slapped it under the stomach, he must have figured that it was not just tired to death but really would stand without hitching. For that Roman-nosed butcher and five dollars, he gave me a wall-eyed pinto with a roached back and thick legs all covered with long hair and a neck like the neck of a camel that you see in the circus. But I knew the points of that breed. It was one hundred percent Indian pony, and that kind are all cut out of one kind of leather.

So I took the pinto. The stable man stood by with a grin to see me saddle and ride my new horse. By that, I could guess that he had given me a bad one, and when I slid into the saddle, the cayuse turned off a barrel full of fireworks. However, I was too busy to be bothered with a bucking horse and I managed to get that idea into his head after a jump or two.

A minute later his hoofs were throwing chunks of snow higher than my head and we were flying out of Marion Crossing on the New Nineveh road. I mean, it was called the road, but anybody who could tell where the road ended and the prairie began was a prophet right enough.

However, I was a pretty good guesser, and that pony was a game one. It hit along about eight miles an hour and stuck there steady as a lock. It slipped in the snow about as much forward as it did back, and *nothing* could put him off his feet.

It was a little after three o'clock, as I was saying, when I started out of Marion Crossing. And it was just half-past eight by my watch when I got into sight of New Nineveh.

Did you ever see any of those pictures of the retreat of the Grand Army—one of those camp pictures where the camp is just a dirty little spot on the snow and the wolves are sneaking around the horizon line?

New Nineveh looked just like that but more so. It was just big enough to be seen, and it was ornery enough to salt down the whole state of heaven, but still it looked pretty fine to me. And when I stood by the hotel stove beating some blood into my hands, I asked one of the men standing around waiting for a job to find him, if there had been any excitement around there lately.

He looked at me, and then he looked away at somebody else.

And a little long-whiskered goat in the corner said: "Nothing has happened in New Nineveh since we was hit by the cyclone.

I hadn't heard of any bad tornado hitting New Nineveh—more was the pity—and so I asked what storm he meant.

He said: "You look around and you'll see some of the marks it left behind pretty fresh still."

Somebody else drawled: "Too damned fresh."

I could see that they were talking around me and that they were saying things that meant a lot more to each other than they did to me. I decided to keep my mouth shut and just listen for a while because when a Westerner doesn't want to be forced, you can't hurry him. Mostly, he's always rushing. But when he decides to go slow, he takes a real ornery pride in his slowness. So I didn't say a thing for a long while, and finally I heard a man say that maybe I would have a chance to take a look at that same cyclone.

I said: "You must be mistaken, partner. I ain't riding a horse of that brand."

He only grinned.

"They're out hunting for this hurricane now, and the boys particular wish to promise that they'll bring him back here in town if they have to bust."

"Somebody has been shooting up the town?" I asked.

And there was a sick feeling inside of me that maybe this would hook up with the kid—that maybe Jigger Bunts was the man that had been trying to wreck New Nineveh. There was one satisfaction—that no matter where he landed with his heels after he jumped into the air in that town, he couldn't fail to hit somebody that needed hitting.

I know a good deal about the brand of man that they had New Nineveh. Once I hired a crew of hands there. But that is another story, as they say. It was nearly the *last* story, I can tell you, so far as I was concerned.

"You are a pretty good guesser," said the chap with the whiskers, who seemed to be the designated talker for the crowd, him being about the hardest-looking case in the lot. "Yes, there has been somebody shooting up the town. A gent with a new way of doing things. He brings in the boys that he has shot up and leaves 'em at the doctor's door while he stands around and waits for more trade. He has a fine, quiet way of working. He uses one sucker for bait to catch the others. He takes in the gents that he has shot up to the town where they have a whole lot of relatives. Understand? And then he goes and

94

gets a room at the hotel for himself and his two guns . . ."

The two guns finished it off for me. I knew that it was the kid who had been at work and I think that was the sickest minute in my life, next to the one in which I read his note to me.

I got the story in pieces and had to patch it together. Some of it may have been exaggerated a little, but, altogether, it made a pretty straight story. What had happened was something like this.

The kid brought that rat, Bud Crandall, into town. A bullet had raked Crandall along the ribs, but he hadn't been hurt so bad that he couldn't ride sixty miles. By the time he got to New Nineveh, he was feeling sick, of course, but he was feeling happy, too, because he knew that he had plenty of friends in that town. There were four cousins of his by name of Askew and Harper in New Nineveh, and as he got to the doctor's house, he sent around word to them that he was in trouble and needed them.

They came in a bunch. You may have noticed that the gang spirit runs pretty high in all crooks like that. They work in bands wherever they can and they make it a point always to hang together. They feel that it's good fellowship. But it isn't. It's just low-down knowing that they may need each other someday. An honest man hates a crowd, but a thug hates to be alone.

95

Of course, when his cousins came, this Crandall lied to them about what had happened.

The doctor heard all about the story that Crandall told, which was that this Bunts had stuck him up while they were riding along side by side, and that Bunts had taken away sixty-five dollars of his money but that he was such a new crook that he thought that was all the money that Crandall had and so he didn't search him any further and didn't get the hundred and eighty dollars besides that Crandall had in his wallet. He said that after the robbery, the kid decided that dead men tell no tales and shot him in cold blood, but when he found that Crandall was not dead, he was afraid to finish the job. The sight of the blood was too much for him. And he started to ride to New Nineveh.

In the light of what followed, you would think that the people in that town might guess that the kid was painted a little blacker than life. But they didn't think. They didn't *like* to think. They told me what a crook and what a coward the kid was just before they went to tell me how he had shot up the whole town. They couldn't put two and two together and see that one half of their yarn spoiled the other half.

However, I didn't point out any of those things to them. I wanted to get the story from them just as they understood it, because I knew that that was the way that it would come to the ears

of the United States police. In a day
yarn would be crystallized and a hu
would be willing to swear to the sam
story.

Well, I got the whole story and it r
better case for the kid than I had exp
the beginning of the yarn.

They said that after the four cousins ɕ
had heard this story of his about th
and the shooting, they asked Cranda
happened that the kid had remained in
after doing a job like this.

When the old goat with the whiske
that point, I held my breath, because I
wondering a good deal on the same pɛ
the answer, according to Crandall, wa
that the kid had done it on a dare.

I could have groaned. Because I knew
was the truth. It was the sort of thing thaᴵ
the Great would have done, and I co
now, that the kid was trying to model
according to the example of the man thɛ
was.

Yes, he had gone to the hotel and got
there as calm as you please and then h
down and got something to eat, and while
eating there, something after midnight, tl
cousins of Crandall came in.

Afterward, I saw them all and you coᴜ
that they were really relations of Crandall

the same yellow skin that came from too
h coffee and tobacco and too little work.
ause work sweats the poison out of a man's
em pretty regularly. They had the same sort
greasy handsome face, too.

ll these men had been raised with guns in
r hands, just the way Crandall had. All of
n packed Colts stuck away in their clothes
ready to come out as slick as a whistle at the
t call on them. And the four of them slouched
to young Jigger Bunts and stood around his
le.

here was an old Negro working as cook at
t hotel and he was the one who had cooked
some ham and coffee for Jigger. Through the
hen door, which he pushed open a peg or
, he saw the whole affair, afraid to keep on
tching, because he knew what was going to
ppen, and a lot too curious to go away. He said
t Jigger sat there as calmly as you please and
nt on eating his supper and looking the four of
m up and down.

f course, I could believe that, and it amused
to think of anyone really trying to stare the
d down. Because he wasn't that kind. His black
es weren't made to droop away under anyone's
re.

Finally the four got tired of waiting for him to
gin to wilt and one of them leaned over and
id: "I think your name is Bunts?"

The kid looked up to him and said: "I'm afraid that you have the advantage of me, sir."

Right there I broke out laughing, and that nearly wrecked the rest of the story.

Chapter Thirteen

Those New Nineveh men stood around and gaped at me, and the chap with the whiskers asked me if I doubted the story, but I told him no, that I didn't.

Matter of fact, I had laughed just because I was hysterical, I suppose, and not because it didn't seem true. Oh, I could understand the thing easy enough. That was the sort of a slicked up remark that Dalfieri would have made in a place like that. So I knew that it was real. But back to the story.

"I am afraid that you have the advantage of me, sir," the kid had said to four thugs standing around waiting for the time to come when they could tear him open and see what made him run!

I laughed, but I could just as easy have groaned.

"It ain't half of the advantage that I'm gonna have," said the other fellow. "Unless you'll stand up and come along with us to a place down the street where you can rest behind some bars and where you'll be watched, so's it can be seen that you have a nice, quiet night's sleep."

The kid nodded and smiled at him. It was Harry Askew that had said that. And when it looked as though Jigger was simply going to give up and go along without a fight—on account of him looking so pleasant—one of the Harper boys (I think it was Steve Harper) had to break in and say that there was one thing before the kid started, and that was for him to hand back the sixty-five dollars that he had stolen from Bud Crandall.

The kid was finishing his coffee. And while the cup was emptying, he chatted with those fellows, and then he said that he didn't mind considering what they had to say to him, but, first off, he would have another cup of hot coffee. He reached for the pot and filled himself a piping hot dose of it in one of those big tin cups that hold nearly a pint.

This was a little too much for the boys. Jud Harper said that they had waited long enough and told the kid to stand up and come with them—and put his hands up over his head while he was standing up out of the chair.

This to Dalfieri! That was all I could think about when I listened to that. Not what the kid would probably do, but what he would think that Dalfieri had ought to do in the same pinch. Something wild and crazy, I had no doubt at all.

He said: "Gentlemen, I want to oblige you, but the fact is that the money which I took from Bud Crandall was taken by him from some friends of mine, and was taken by him through dirty card tricks. Whereas, what I used to take the money back again was a perfectly clean gun."

"Cover him . . . he means trouble, boys!" said

the Askew brother named Sim, and fetched out a pair of Colts.

And the rest of that bunch started for their guns at the same minute, and the cook blinked, getting ready for the roar of guns. When he opened his eyes again, he saw the kid throw that cup of hot coffee—boiling hot—right into the faces of the gang.

Sim Askew let off both his guns—and blew two little holes in the ceiling—and sent one of those slugs through the boot of a fellow who was sleeping over the dining room.

Sim was the only one who had had time to get his guns out, and he was so burned with coffee that all he could do after that was to hop around and yell for help and say that he was blinded. Matter of fact, he was badly burned, and when I saw his face, it looked as though it had been rubbed on an emery wheel. It was a sight, I can tell you.

His brother Harry was scalded, too, and so was Jud Harper, though not so bad. The only one that wasn't pretty much hurt was Steve Harper, and before he got his guns to working, the kid had come out of his chair with a leap and smashed a fist into Steve's face.

I didn't have to ask whether Steve did much fighting after that. I just had to remember those big, thick, flexible shoulders of the kid, and the way the cords stood out on his wrists like hamstrings. I knew that Steve Harper must have gone down with a whack. And that was exactly what he did. He slammed his head on the floor so hard that he couldn't get up without help five minutes later, when the old cook came out and dragged him up to his feet.

In the meantime, the kid had gone out of that dining room in about two jumps and slammed the door behind him. The whole hotel was buzzing like a nest of wasps right away. The town always slept with one ear open for gun plays. And when the guns started, it got up *pronto*, because there is no fun in being shot while you're lying in bed.

Well, between you and me, that was about the size of most of the gunfights out West when it was wild and wooly, as they say. Revolvers were the fashion, and revolvers, by my way of thinking, were always a mighty silly weapon. Exceptions, of course. Here and there you'd meet somebody like Billy the Kid. But the exceptions just proved the rule that in a revolver fight those that got hurt were usually the bystanders.

Here was a good case in point. Four men, all handy with their guns, come in and stand right around the table where the kid was eating his supper. They tell him to hold up his hands, and one of the four gets out two guns and covers him—and yet he gets away without so much as firing a shot!

You may say that the coffee was an extra card

in the pack. But where you're talking about a brave man, you'll find that he usually can find a joker in the pack. I used to know a brakeman who worked in the West for years and he never packed a gun in all his life and yet he was being hunted all the time by hobos that he had kicked off the trains, here and there. Nothing mysterious about how he handled them. He used to walk up to the yeggs and take their guns away from them and stick them down their throats. He had a pair of hard fists and he kept the knuckles all calloused with knocking down "killers." The point was that he never took them serious, and I suppose that nobody could do much in the way of being *bad* if he had an audience that was laughing at him.

Anyway, there was the kid out of the dining room without a scratch on him.

The people in the hotel spilled out into the street as fast as they could run, waving their guns, because the four cousins were raising a terrible yell and saying that there was a murderer and a crook that had just got away. And the boys swarmed out and some of them grabbed horses and the rest of them started tearing off on foot, because as a rule the boys in New Nineveh never overlooked a chance to blaze away at a living target.

And here came the joke. This was the thing that the old fellow with the whiskers couldn't repeat without nearly choking to death, it made him so mad. This was the thing that made New Nineveh blush for years afterward, just thinking about it. Because they prided themselves on their hardness, that town did. And they had all rushed out, waving their guns, to get this fresh eighteen-year-old kid.

And while they were still rushing, guns were booming on the edge of the town, where they were shooting at every shadow that looked like a man. In fact a calf was killed. While all that was going on, down the stairs of the hotel walks Jigger Bunts!

Yes, sir, though it is hard to believe that any *real* man would do such a thing, it was exactly the sort of a thing that Dalfieri would have done, of course.

He wouldn't allow a crowd of gunfighters to disturb him any. He wouldn't get flustered and put ill at ease. Not Dalfieri! He would go right along his own sweet way. Because he was a gentleman, and a gentleman doesn't let himself get flustered by a lot of ruffians like the New Ninevites.

No, when he went out of that dining room, he simply had walked upstairs and went into his room, and he didn't run out of the hotel at all!

Up in his room, you see, he had left a lot of his things, including his hat. And could you imagine Dalfieri running away from a fight without his hat?

No, you couldn't. Not if you had sat in at the birth and the making of Dalfieri the way I had done.

Up there in his room the kid took plenty of time and rolled up some blankets which he thought he might need, and left a little note written out to the proprietor, promising to pay for those blankets the first time that he got a chance.

When he was good and ready, he took his roll of blankets and his hat and went downstairs, and *walked* out of the hotel, right past two or three dozen blockheads that were running around raving for him. But they swore afterward that they were looking for a poor scared critter that would be running and ducking from one cover to another, and they never even so much as looked twice at a man that was walking—with a blanket roll under his arm!

He went right out into the stable. He led out his horse—doesn't it seem too plain idiotic that nobody had thought of looking for his horse?—and after he had saddled that horse, he jogged it out into the main street of New Nineveh!

I suppose that New Nineveh would have paid thousands of dollars if it didn't have to admit that he was able to do that and get away with it. But that wasn't all that he did. It was not half!

When he got about two-thirds of the way down the street, three men ran up to him with their guns and hollered out to know who he was.

And he stopped his horse and said: "I am Jeremy Bunts. Do you want me?"

There is no doubt about it. That was exactly what he did. And those three men stood there as if they were paralyzed, and finally he spoke to his horse and rode right on through the three of them!

That's another thing that may be hard to believe. But it was done. Those three were as brave as lions until they heard the voice of Jigger, and then there was something in that voice that made them curl up inside and froze up their talking muscles.

It has happened to me, for that matter.

But oh, if they had only kept paralyzed! But they didn't!

Chapter Fourteen

I suppose that Jigger's voice and the size of his shoulders and the way he had of sitting in the saddle, as if it was a throne, was too much for them. But the minute that they saw his back, they was stimulated a lot and remembered how brave they was—and that they were looking for this very man. And I suppose they remembered, too, that there were three of them and that there was only one of him. It must have been a comforting thought, too!

They didn't run after him. They got their guns up, and then they yapped at him to turn around and come back, or they would drill him, just as sure as the devil!

You or me or anybody else would have dropped down low in the saddle and seen how quick our spurs could have turned the walk of that horse into a gallop. But you gotta remember that there wasn't any real human being in that saddle. There was Dalfieri—the man that never was!

And the kid—or rather Dalfieri—did exactly what they told him to do. That is, he turned that horse of his clear around and started toward the three.

"Stick up your hands!" they yelled at him.

And he stuck up his hands, but he stuck them up with a gun in each of them. Also, when he came, he came at a hard gallop, with his horse just fair legging it along. And he blazed away at them.

They had a man on horseback to shoot at, and he only had a group of men on foot. But their nerves were a little upset and his were—well, the nerves of Dalfieri.

There is no use making a long story out of it. He simply shot down every one of those three men.

I have a paper here beside me now, with the account of that shooting. Here is the list that it gives.

Richard Hughes, of Belfast, Ireland,
   31 years old.
Frederick Ginsing, of Hamburg, Germany,
   22 years old.
Bartholomew Lewis, of Boston, Mass.,
   24 years old.

Hughes was shot through the hip and the ball traveled around inside the hip bone and came up in the small of the back where it lodged under the skin and could be seen with the naked eye—a little bluish lump there. The doctor just cut the skin and the slug fell out in his hands. Hughes had a lot the worst wound. He was in bed for weeks before he could sit up, and it was thought for a while that he was going to die. But men took a lot of killing in those days.

Frederick Ginsing, the German with a little withered arm, was one of these fellows who look prematurely born and never stop looking that way as long as they live. He had a collar bone broken, and the bullet went right on, glancing up through the thick flesh at the base of the neck. But the top of the lung was missed and there were no big arteries severed. So he was all right in a short time.

Bart Lewis, of Boston, got it through the thigh, a nice clean hole that didn't even scrape the thigh bone. He said that all he felt was a numbness, at first. He didn't know where he was hit, until he tried to take a step, and then he fell flat on his face.

What was plain was that they had not hurt the kid. They had sent enough lead in his general direction, but they had scored no hits. He rode right on!

Yes, anybody else, of course, would have snapped his horse around and rode for dear life, but Dalfieri, having been turned in his course, kept right on in the same direction.

People heard the shooting and came tearing down the street, and a dozen of them meeting the kid, said: "What's happened?"

What do you think he said?

Why, he told them the truth, of course! That was Dalfieri's way.

He said: "Bunts has just shot three men, down there. They tried to stop him."

The crowd spilled down that way, by horse and foot. And when they got there, they found Ginsing sitting up, yelling and cursing at them for a lot of fools and cowards and telling them to go back and take the man that had just rode through them, because that was Jigger Bunts, or the devil in that shape!

They were a good deal bewildered at this, and somebody said that Ginsing was raving, and that it couldn't have been Jigger Bunts, because he was just jogging his horse along, slow and easy— and heading right through the town.

Ginsing began to scream at them, but I suppose they never would have paid any attention to him, he was so excited, but here Bart Lewis broke in and told them that it was Bunts that had just passed through the lot of them.

By that time, he was out of sight down the street, and they grabbed their horses and went down the street like mad.

They didn't find him. He had turned off the main street right in the middle of town. A woman whose husband was away working in the mines had heard the racket in the town and had got up and dressed hurriedly, and while she was looking out the window, she saw a fellow who answered the description of Jigger Bunts and his horse. He was still just jogging his horse along, slow and easy. She could see him pretty clear, because although there was a film of clouds across the sky, there was a big moon behind them, and so against the white of the snow, you could make out things pretty good. The snowstorm hadn't hit over by New Nineveh yet.

She said afterward that when she saw him trotting along so cool and comfortable, she told herself that there was at least *one* calm, sensible man who wanted to keep out of the way of trouble in New Nineveh.

That's the way things go in real life.

There was no reason why Jigger should have got away that night if he had acted like any normal human being. But he didn't act like any human being for the pretty simple reason that what he was modeling himself after was a man that never was. Jigger Bunts would have wanted to run like anybody else, when the time came, but he had to be Dalfieri.

While the men and the horses were washing up and down the main street of New Nineveh, the kid was tracking off through the snow as easy as you please until they got to work and began to organize a little and search the houses, thinking that in some way he must have tried to hide himself in one of the sheds, or even in one of the houses.

It was when they began to search the houses that they came across the miner's wife. When she told them about the man she had seen, and when she gave them all the particulars of just how he looked and just how his horse looked, they realized who it was that she had seen and they went after him pelting, you had better believe.

However, by this time he had a cool hour's lead on them, and even if he hadn't rushed his horse, he was sure to be at least five miles away from the town, which makes for a long and a hard chase. Besides, the kid was not taking any chances.

The New Nineveh men got a couple of hours away from town and they came across a house with a light in it. There they found a man who was up and dressed and cleaning his rifle and very hot about a thing that had happened to him a while before.

His name was Wilbur Green and he was squatting on a nice piece of land with plenty of water and pretty good grass, where he was trying to raise cows and a few horses, and doing pretty good at it. He said that a knock had come at his door, and when he called out, a man asked to talk to him. He said what about, and the man said that he wanted to make a horse swap with him. Green got up and went to the door and didn't forget to take a gun along with him, because a gun was apt to be handy in a little midnight chat like this.

The stranger said that he had a pretty good horse, which he had left in the corral, and he had taken in exchange for it a horse which he had found there. Green said that it was the best horse in the bunch he owned, and I don't doubt that it was, because the kid had a pretty good eye for horseflesh. Green started raising quite a holler and even waved his gun a little, but the kid told him to put the gun down, and said that he had hurt enough men for one night and didn't want to have anything more on his conscience. Green didn't make any bones about saying that he was afraid to tackle the kid single-handed. And I don't blame him. Fighting power just breathes out of some men like the smell out of a flower. The kid admitted that he was getting the best of the trade and he said that he would come back and give the stranger all the money that was coming to him for boot in the trade. In the meantime, he didn't have any cash and he would have to make Green trust him.

Green was not feeling trusting, though. And now he had the second best of his string saddled and his Winchester oiled up and ready for use, when the gang from New Nineveh came along. Green dismounted and led the men into his house to have coffee and cold bread while he told them what had happened. Then they hit the saddle and went on.

Two of the men turned back though, at this

point, and it was from them that the town had been able to get all the news that had circulated about the trail as far as Greens's house.

This was the story that the old goat with the whiskers told me in the hotel there at New Nineveh, and you can imagine that, while he told me, I was not feeling none too happy, because any fool with half an eye could have told that it was my dirty work which was ruining things. Being Dalfieri so hard had cost the kid four wounded men, even if they weren't kin of Crandall.

And every one of those four wounded men had friends.

In those days, it was almost better to kill a man than to wound him. If you killed a man, his friends put him under the ground, and after he was buried, they were usually too much bothered with troubles of their own to trouble much about trying to do anything for him.

But if a man was just wounded, say, he never let his partners forget the other fellow who had been on the lucky end of that shooting party. So you might say that the kid had worked himself up four sets of trouble that were sure to last him for quite a while. That was not counting the three that he had scalded and the one that he had knocked down.

But if there is any difference between a bullet wound and being scalded I should say that it is all in favor of the bullet.

Being shot is sort of honorable, but being knocked down or scalded, is just foolish and makes everybody laugh at you.

There was plenty more talk in New Nineveh, but I had heard enough, and I knew what I had to do.

Chapter Fifteen

When I said that New Nineveh was full of nothing but crooks and such, I forgot one man. And I remembered him right at this point, when I heard the old goat finish up with his story. There was Judge Henry Dahlgren in town. He was a *real* judge back East someplace. I mean, he was still on the bench, but he was taking a vacation here where he could shoot deer and such, and have a fine rough time. Some men get a funny sort of pleasure out of making themselves uncomfortable. But anyway, the judge was a white man. He was extra white.

I got out of that hotel and buzzed straight for the judge and got there just in time to head him off as he was starting on a hunting trip.

I started right in begging him to give me some advice because I was in a lot of trouble, and I told him that I wanted to find some way of helping the kid.

"Young Bunts," said the judge, "is the man who shot up the town last night. Is he not?"

I said that he was, but I started to explain when the judge, he cut in on me and said: "Is the boy really all right?"

I started to explain again, but the judge just

117

said: "Tell me yes or no. It's your opinion that I want, and not your evidence."

So I said yes.

"Well," said the judge, "you may have noticed that this boy has not actually *killed* anyone?"

I said, of course, that I was glad that that was the case.

"But," said the judge, "that would not keep him from a pretty severe sentence in the East. And I suppose the rascal should get a severe sentence in any part of the civilized world. However, this part of the world is not yet civilized. Selfishly, I am glad of it. And I think that if he were to stop his wildness for a while, and live quietly, this affair would blow over."

He went on to say that when the wounds of the hurt men had been healed and a little time had passed, what the kid had done would not seem so very wild and people wouldn't call him a badman unless he went right on letting blood.

That was logical. There was no doubt about that. The judge said the thing for me to do was to get the kid to leave the area, and to get enough money to him so that he could pay for what he needed to live on. I swore to the judge that I would like nothing better than a chance to help the kid. Also, I said that the kid was the most honest man that I had ever known.

The judge didn't smile. He was not that sort of a man. He looked you in the eye as serious as you please and he never seemed to make up his mind by guesswork. You could see how wonderful square he was. I made up my mind that if I ever got into a scrape and if I was on the right side of the law, it would be worth traveling three thousand miles just to be judged by him, and if I was in the wrong, it was worth traveling thirty thousand miles to keep away from him.

He told me in concluding: "You paint a very rosy picture of this boy. But perhaps you're right. He's simply enthusiastic . . . not a criminal. Well, if he's as honest as you say that he is, he will probably try to live up to his word and he will do his best to get honest money, if he has any in the world, and use it to pay for that roll of blankets he stole from the hotel and that horse which he took from the rancher, Green. But, sir, *has* he such a thing as money of his own? And where would he get it?"

It let in a very welcome ray of light upon my wits. Of course there was money owing to him. He had at least wages for three months due to him. And if that was not enough, I knew that, among us, my men and I could take care of him, and be very glad to do it. And as for where he would go to get that money, why, there was not a bit of doubt of that. He would ride straight back to the ranch and there he would ask for what was due to him.

I could have cursed myself for not thinking of

that before. But that's the way of it when a man is in a bit of trouble—his brain seems to get all filled with rust, if you know what I mean.

I got on my horse and started for the ranch again. But I was fagged out. I had missed a night's sleep and I had traveled more than a hundred and forty miles without closing my eyes and with all sorts of trouble hounding me every step of the way. So that I found that I simply could not sit in the saddle. I would find that my head was on my chest every minute or two, and then I would wake up with a start, half slide out of the saddle and that pinto starting to buck.

I got down and made myself a bed with my big rubber poncho and my blankets. I threw the reins of the horse and I rolled up in the blankets and hoped that that bronco might be somewhere in sight when I opened my eyes again.

I could not keep up any longer. No, sir, I was so beat that I had to get that sleep.

I was somewhere around thirty miles from the Bar L outfit's place when I lay down. And that must have been about noon in the day. It was around four or five when I started up out of that sleep with my heart beating like mad.

There was nothing to be afraid of near me, and my horse was fairly handy. In five minutes I was in the saddle again, but something told me that I should have no luck out of the trip.

I rode right on at a good stiff pace. That pinto

was mean and had a gait all full of jars and jolts, but, just the same, he was a steady traveler and he had the toughness of his breed. I headed on for the ranch. I landed there about an hour after dusk had turned into the full dark of the night.

I got down from the pinto, knowing that he would never be worth a pinch of salt after that day's ride, but I hardly cared. I was too full of gloom, because with the wind singing in my ears and freezing in my face, I was surer than ever that I had ridden out to the ranch on a fool's chase.

But it *wasn't* a fool's chase. It was only because I had had that sleep that I had missed out. If I had been like the kid, made up of nothing but nerve and iron, I would have been able to do my work well enough. But I was never made out of such stuff. I never would pretend to imitate Dalfieri, not even for a minute.

When I came into the old ranch house, I saw Chick Murphy and old Parkhurst sitting by the kitchen stove. I gave them one look and then I knew that nothing but bad news was in the place for me.

I didn't even speak to them, but started on through for the dining room, where I could hear somebody shuffling around.

I had my hand on the door when one of the boys sang out softly that I had better not go in there.

I turned around and came back to the stove and

spread out my hands over the top of it. But it was not that kind of warmth that I needed. And the two of them sat there like owls, hugging their knees and staring at me.

Then I yelled at them all at once: "Damn your necks, why don't you blat it out and get it done with?"

They weren't the best-tempered pair in the world, but they just turned their heads and looked at one another and started staring at me again. And I saw what was worse than anything—that there was pity in their eyes. I turned around and started for the door again.

And then Chick said: "Don't go in, boss. Old Wong is in there, trying to lay out the body more natural and make it look more like it's alive."

It knocked me all galley west. I grabbed at the wall and held myself up and I managed to ask them if it was the kid that was lying dead in there.

That brightened them up a little bit. They said that it wasn't the kid.

"It's only a dead man that he's left there," said Parkhurst.

Yes, I was too late by more than an hour and a half. The kid had killed his man, at last, and I knew that there wasn't much hope for him. Not with his spirit. The boys told me that a man they didn't know had ridden up to the ranch house along about suppertime, and they had let him in and he had told them about all the hell that the kid had raised in New Nineveh that night before.

They were about through supper when the door opened and there stood the kid, laughing and happy to be back, and singing out: "Hello, fellows!"

When the stranger heard that voice, he turned around in his chair, snaking out a gun as he turned, and he tried to sink a bullet in the kid, but he only split the door. And the kid's gun snapped out very pretty, and the stranger rolled over on the floor with a slug of lead in his brains. The kid stood there, looking at this dead face on the floor for a minute, and then he backed out the door without saying another word. When they got their wits about them, they ran out to call him. But there was no sight or sound of him again!

They knew what I knew as they told me, that it was the kid's last try to come back to an honest living. After that, there was nothing left for him except what lay outside of the law, which is a pretty wild and cold country for an eighteen-year-old boy. Oh, the three of us were a sick and sad group thinking of it, and of the kid, and of all the good times we had had that winter, laughing at his poor, fool, innocent ways.

I went into the dining room.

It was Steve Harper! He must have had a bright thought earlier in the day and figured things out just the way that the judge had figured them out for me—except that Steve only wanted to get his chance to drive a bullet through the innards of Jigger Bunts.

Well, that was the end of Steve, and, in a way, it was the end of the kid. And we would never again see a body so brave and gentle and willing and kind and foolish. Even old Wong knew it.

Wong was still fussing around. He had made that dead man look mighty natural. I guess he must have worked pretty hard getting the ache out of his heart and trying to undo what the kid had done. Like a child trying to fix a toy that somebody else has put his heel right on.

When he saw me, as though he knew that him and me had been special fond of the kid, he shoved his hands inside of his coat sleeves and stood there, looking down at the floor, and crying.

And I said: "Damn your hide, what good can that do?"

Then I sneaked off into the night, where the air was fresher.

PART TWO

Maybelle

Chapter Sixteen

Months had passed. I was sitting with my head in my hands. I was feeling so low that I could have stood up and walked under a snake without scratching its stomach. I was feeling so small that I could have used the shell of a hickory nut for house and barn.

Sam Mitchell came in from the bunkhouse.

"How's things, chief?" he asked.

"Damn your hide," I said. "Don't talk to me!"

He picked up the paper where it had fallen on the floor and he read the article out loud, spelling the words to himself before he pronounced them. Because Mitchell never had no educational advantages, like me.

This was what he read out loud to me, and every word made me sicker and sicker.

FAMOUS OUTLAW HOLDS UP
NEW NINEVEH STAGE
OUTFACES THREE GUARDS
AND ESCAPES WITH LOOT

Last night, under a full moon, the celebrated bandit, Jigger Bunts, waited in a gap of the Nineveh Mountains until the New Nineveh coach came through and then stepped out with a rifle to . . .

"Shut up!" I yelled at Mitchell.

He went on running his eyes through the column as fast as he could, bringing out important words, here and there.

"Three guards . . . a sawed-off shotgun . . . lady fainted . . . when last seen riding west . . . Dog-gone me, Tom, it looks like he might be heading for *us*. Might be coming back to pay us a visit. That would be pretty good, eh?"

"Shut up," I said. "I've been thinking too much for my peace of mind!"

Just then the cook came in.

"Hey, Wong," says Mitchell, "Jigger is drifting back this way. You savvy? The kid . . . maybe he's coming back to pay us a visit!"

"Kid come? By golly!" Wong exclaimed, and he looked at us with eyes as big as saucers and a grin that tickled both ears. The kid was still the favorite with Wong. He'd always man-aged to shy the best chuck onto the kid's plate, back when Jigger was working with us on the ranch.

But it didn't cheer me up much to see Wong's face. I could only groan as I said to Mitchell: "Maybe Jigger is coming, and if he does, I want you to tell me how we're going to be able to do something for him . . . how're we're gonna be able to stop him, Sam, before he goes on with this bandit work of his long enough to jam his head right into a hangman's noose."

ose miserable
to get away
y for me to
to be done in

ns hitched to
e long trail.
ng. All of the
etter done in
New Nineveh
his morning.
neriness and
itted into my
and I busted
ckskins with
their mouths
t a man will

th two horses
ed them into
t the hotel.
pect in New
where some
g a lot over
ned to them
ent stamping
the door of
and used up
while they
inking that I

responded, very

Steve Harper.
ught of him in
ere, incidentally
art enough to be
der instead of for
he killings would
hings kept up the
had to admit that
tside right away,
g that the puzzle

at was right and
course, the fool
he wrong course
le I was the boss
it was justice that
is thing, it didn't
oticed that the hat
o small when you

and looked the
day—oh, what a
high gray clouds
he cows had their
blowing their tails
the yearlings were
ropping their heads
winter had come

already. Somehow, the sight of th[e]
cows was too much for me. I ha[d]
from the ranch, and it was eas[y]
remember a lot of things that ough[t]
town.

So I had a tough pair of bucksk[in]
the buckboard and I started out on t[he]

I'll tell you how mean I was feeli[ng]
errands that I had to do would be [in]
Marion Crossing, of course. But [I]
had the call over the good town
I think that the lowness and the o[ld]
the meanness of New Nineveh just
own mind like clockwork, that day.
off down the trail, popping the b[ull]
the whip one minute and sawing on
with the reins the next, the way th[at]
do when he's too down to be decent

I got into New Nineveh at dark, wi[th]
pretty near too tired to step. I shov[ed]
the livery stable and got me a room

Of course, I had what you'd half e[xpect]
Nineveh—a room right over anothe[r]
gents were playing poker and argui[ng]
their cards and their liquor. I liste[ned]
yapping for a long time, and then I w[ent]
down the stairs and I kicked open
their room. I leaned in the doorway
a few minutes passing bad languag[e]
sat pretty dumbstruck and scared, th[en]

must be nothing less than a deputy sheriff or a celebrated gunfighter, by the proud talk that I was using.

"Now, you sons of goats, you tin-horn cheapskates, you corn-fed flatheads, you loud-mouthed loafers, if I hear another peep out of you during the night, I'll come down here and chaw you up so damned small and fine that you'll blow away in the first night wind. You hear me yap and remember!"

I give the door another kick and went back to my own room.

You would think, maybe, that I was a pretty high and hardy fellow, by that line of talk that I used, but I wasn't. I'm harmless, most generally, but when I get depressed it acts bad on me—like low-grade whiskey, and comes out in wrong language and such things. You understand how it is.

These fellows thought that I was some terrible fighter, and they didn't let out a peep.

Just the same, I couldn't sleep any. I lay in bed a while glorying in how I had bluffed out those pikers. But then I began to remember about the kid, and that took the joy out quick. All these time since he was cut loose and started burning up atmosphere and crowding the headlines of the newspapers, I had figured that someday, somehow, I would have to work things so that this here Jigger Bunts would be tamed down and made safe for democracy. But I never could figure it out no way at all. Planning on how to handle Jigger was like planning on how to handle the next comet that heaves into sight. You may do a lot of looking and you may do a lot of thinking, but by the time you get turned around, the comet has gone kiting through another dozen light years, and you got to adjust your thinking all over again.

Just before dawn, I *did* fall asleep, and it was well after sunup when I awakened, and that gave me a guilty feeling to start the day. I had breakfast, feeling more grouchier than ever. Then I started out to get my errands done and when I was coming out of a harness shop after having a fight about the price of some saddlebags, I hear a girl sing out: "Hello, Tommy! What's the good news?"

There ain't much that makes me any madder than to be called Tommy. I don't know why. It's all right for a nickname. Only it don't fit in with my idea of myself. I always imagine that name going with blue eyes and pink cheeks. Besides, when a man is running a big ranch and gets to be forty years old, he's got a right to be a little particular about his moniker.

I turned around with a growl and there was Maybelle Crofter, sashaying across the street and waving her hand at me. She looked more pretty than ever, which might've come of her wearing a blue jacket and a blue skirt, and with a big twist of her hair coming over her shoulder and hanging down in a pigtail. It was like the outfit of a sixteen-year-old girl. Well, Maybelle—or Mabel, to spell it the right way and the easier way—could *look* sixteen when she chose to. She was every inch of thirty-one, but that didn't bother her. When she felt extra young, she could dress extra young. And when she felt old, she could dress herself up and look like the mother of a family on her way to church. Which I suppose that Maybelle never seen the inside of a church in her whole life.

As I was saying, this girl comes sashaying across the street waving her hand at me, and she comes up and she says: "The finest sight I've seen since I had measles, Tommy?"

Some of my grouch melted out of me. She had a sunny pair of eyes, that kid did. I knew that there was tons of bad in her. Everybody else knew that, too. But I knew that there was good, too. Anyway, she was company above the average of what you get in New Nineveh.

I said: "What dropped you in this dive, Maybelle? Have you gone and got yourself another husband?"

"That's what I ain't done nothing but," Maybelle said. "I got me a fine six foot, two or three inches of husband."

"He may be big," I said, "but if he lives in New Nineveh, he ain't fine. You take it from me, will you?"

"I know," Maybelle said. "This town is full of pikers and strong arm blackjacks, all right."

"What might be the moniker of the guy that you caught, Maybelle?"

"Harry Wayne is his name," she answered.

"Hey!" I replied. "Harry Wayne? The rancher? How did you ever pick up anything as good as that, kid?"

"Don't be nasty, Tommy," Maybelle said, getting a little cold. "I don't mind an old friend speaking his mind, but I'm not such a piker, when you come to look me over!" She picked up her head and dropped a hand on one hip and did a pirouette very slow. "How am I?" Maybelle asked.

I had to admit that she was pretty, though she wasn't half so pretty as she looked. It's not just a beautiful face that can poison men and make them mad for a woman. It's something inside the soul of a girl.

"How do you do it, Maybelle?" I asked. "You've traveled some, but you don't look as though you've as much as gone across the street."

"I don't take things to heart," says Maybelle. "When some folks make a slip, they write it down in red and study that passage a lot. But I . . . well, I just tear out the page."

And she laughed and shook her head. She had a fine laugh. Hearty as a man's, but musical, you know.

"Which husband is this?" I asked her.

"Five," says Maybelle. "Six, I mean to say."

"You sort of lose the count?" I ask.

"I never had much education," Maybelle said, and grinned.

"Well," says I, "how comes it that Harry Wayne is letting you drift around by yourself like this? Is he in town buying cattle, or something?"

"Oh, no," she said, "he's back in Nevada getting a fresh start."

I asked her what she meant.

"He came across one of my back trails," said Maybelle. "And he read the sign of a lot of my scandals. You would never think that a fellow like Harry Wayne would have thin skin. But he has. He made a scene and I had to tell him where to get off. So he grabbed the Overland and . . . Hello, Missus Gunther!"

A lady was heading down the street, and as she came past us, she slowed up enough to look the pair of us over, then she stuck her head in the air and went sailing on. It was easy to see by that that Maybelle's reputation had come to town with her, at last, but it didn't bother Maybelle none.

"Missus Gunther is hard of hearing," Maybelle said loud enough for Mrs. Gunther to hear. "The years will tell, won't they?"

And you could see a shiver run through Mrs. Gunther's back as she went huffing down the sidewalk.

Chapter Seventeen

"Well," I said, when I got through laughing, "you're after alimony now, I suppose?"

"Sure," Maybelle said. "By reason of not causing hubby any bother about this reason, I get a pretty good slice off the estate. When the dough arrives, I get myself a vacation."

"Vacation!" I said. "Why, honey, you've had nothing but vacations since they tried to keep you in school back in home!"

"Don't make me think back that far," Maybelle replied. "It gives me a headache. I never remember anything before the time when I crowded a few extra letters into my name. But it hasn't been all a vacation. Ask any married woman if it's easy. And I've been married five times . . . six, I mean. When I get my money, I'm going to get me a shack in the mountains where there's nothing nearer to men than grizzly bears and mountain lions. That's the way that I feel."

"You've got enough scalps to retire on," I admitted. "So long, Maybelle."

"Wait a minute," she said. "Take off your pack and rest a while. What's gone wrong on the ranch?"

"Damn the cows and the ranch," I say. "This is about a man, old-timer, and you can't help."

"Can't I?" she said. "Why, young fellow, I'm a professor in just that line of work. Tell Aunt Maybelle what's on your mind. You look like a Methodist Sunday."

I gave her another look. It wasn't that I really expected any solution from her. But I needed help so bad that I was willing to tell everybody how low I felt.

We were standing in front of a house with a *For Rent* sign pasted inside the window. We sat down on the front steps.

"You haven't been here long," I said, "but you've heard about Jigger Bunts?"

She showed life right away.

"The bandit? I know about him, of course."

"But you don't know much, and nobody does except me and a few of the boys out at my ranch. If that bandit showed out there, do you know what way we'd act?"

"Like the rest of the poor fish around here every time they hear his name mentioned," said Maybelle. "You'd dive through the window or anywhere to get clear of him."

"You're wrong, kid," I said. "We'd shake hands all around, get out our best moon-shine whiskey, and pull up an easy chair in front of the fire."

She blinked at me. "Since when have they had easy chairs on a ranch?" she asked.

"Don't get too literal," I said. "I say that Jigger

Bunts is the best-liked kid that was ever on that ranch."

"Did you say 'kid'?" she said.

"He's about twenty," I tell her.

She put up her head and whistled.

"Let me tell you the story all in a nutshell," I went on.

"I was drumming up a crew last fall for riding range on that ranch . . . which is the meanest bit of range in the world . . . and I picked up this Jigger Bunts. Old Sam Mitchell . . . the hound . . . had filled this tenderfoot Bunts full of talk about me. Told him that I once killed six or seven Indians in a fight . . ."

"Six or seven?" gasped Maybelle.

"Sure," I said. "And the kid swallowed even that. He's a fool about such stuff. He was going around looking for a hero, and Mitchell elected me to be the goat, you understand? I took this kid out on the ranch and he went around worshipping me, wearing his clothes like me, and practicing with his Colt day and night to make himself half as good a shot as he thought I must be. And I got tired of the ruction, though it was keeping the whole crew of hands amused all winter long. Well, there were a lot of pictures of actresses and whatnot on the wall of that ranch house . . ."

Maybelle yawned. "I know," she said. "Men are a silly lot of tramps . . . thank God. Go on!"

"One of these blew down, and on the inside

scrap of paper there was a picture of a fancy-looking guy with a short black moustache waxed out at the ends and a flowing necktie, and all the rest. Louis Dalfieri was the name that was under the picture. And the idea come to me that it would be a grand joke to break the kid of worshipping me and start him to worshipping that ham movie actor. So that's what I done. I told him one night how I had been licked fair and square by a man smaller than myself, and when he wouldn't believe it, I pointed to the picture of Louis Dalfieri and told him that that was the man. It was a terrible shock to Jigger Bunts."

"It was a great gag," Maybelle commented. "Go on."

"We started in, then . . . all of us . . . to telling Jigger what a terrible fighter and wonderful outlaw this Louis Dalfieri was. Oh, we worked that idea to the queen's taste, understand? We told him how Dalfieri thought nothing of walking into a barroom and holding up the whole crowd . . . just for the sake of making the bartender set up the drinks. And how Dalfieri took from the rich and give to the poor. You see, we made a sort of a new Robin Hood out of that Dalfieri for the benefit of the kid. And he fell for the whole idea. In a day or so, he'd started in dressing himself up like Dalfieri's picture and . . ."

"The little fool!" Maybelle exclaimed.

"No," I said, pretty serious. "That's where you

139

are wrong . . . he ain't a fool. And if you want proof, I'll point you out to my gang on the ranch . . . all hard-boiled . . . and every one of them would die for the sake of that same kid. The most cheerfulest, best-natured, happy, smiling, willing kid that ever chopped wood for the fire on a snowy morning. Never seen anybody so willing to do a double share of work if he thought that it would help out a pal. A clean sport . . . white all the way through. But the trouble was that he carried his imitation too far, and after a while just dressing the part of Dalfieri wouldn't be enough for him. And the result was that he started on the road. And when he goes cavorting around the mountains, holding folks up, and such things, he's not being himself. He's just aping Louis Dalfieri . . . his idea of a hero. You see?"

Maybelle, she sat there with her eyes closed and her face wrinkled up with pain.

"Oh, don't I understand," she said in a sort of a whisper. "Trying to be somebody else . . . trying to be somebody else."

"Don't cry about it, Maybelle," I said.

"I'm not crying," she says. "It just hurts too much for tears and that's all. Why, Tommy, there's only one thing in the world for you to do."

"Go on, Solomon," I said. "You can show me how to get Jigger out of this mess, I'll be your slave for life. Because I got him into it in the first place."

"Shut up," Maybelle said. "I thought I had the right idea, but it slipped away from me. Lemme think!" She sat there with her face in a knot.

Pretty soon she begins: "This here is gonna give me wrinkles bad." And then: "Tommy, what you got to do is to give this young fool something to be a knight about that is harmless to the rest of the world. You understand?"

"No," I said frankly. "I don't."

"Why, what does a knight do?" Maybelle asks. "He goes around and fights dragons. And then he takes a day off and guards a treasure or something, or carts a message from one king to the next, in spite of the wizards and all such. Have you forgotten the fairy stories?"

It began to dawn on me. But still it wasn't clear.

"Give him something to guard," she said. "Something that really ain't in any danger. You see? Or has he raised so much trouble that the law won't let him alone? Has he killed men?"

"Only one," I told her, "and that was a low-down head-hunter that needed killing. No, I think that the kid has a lot more friends than he has enemies. But he couldn't show his face in public, you know."

She nodded, still biting her lip and thinking. "You said he was twenty?" she asked finally.

"Yea."

"A baby!" she cried.

"Not a baby, either," I began, "but a hundred percent . . ."

"Shut up!" Maybelle hisses. "All men are babies . . . and spoiled ones, too!" Then she says: "I'll tell you what, Tommy, that boy needs a woman and he needs her quick. No mere man could handle him. If he's the sort of fire that you describe, the thing for you to do is to get hold of a mighty safe, mighty sweet girl with a level head on her shoulders and let him start guarding her, if he can. I gather it won't make much difference even if there's nothing to guard her from. You can just *tell* him that there is. Since you've started him into trouble with your lies, you'll have to pull him out of danger again with more lies."

It sounded like sense. It hit me where I lived. I had to get up and walk around, exclaiming: "Maybelle, I think that you've hit the nail on the head, maybe! I feel that you've come close to it. But still, there's something wrong. He's got to have something to worship as well as something to guard. He's got to think that he's taking care of something that is really taking care of him."

She nodded. "You get me perfect," Maybelle said.

"But," I said, "how are you going to make him think that there's any danger at all in the way of one of these Western girls? A girl in this country never has anything to fear from men. Besides, no girl young enough and decent enough to make a wife for him would have the brains to handle him, and if there was any mistake made in the handling of that bunch of lightning, believe me, it would make an explosion that would just blast a few lives to hell and back again, and make no mistake about that! This kid is the concentrated essence of dynamite."

"Well, you want him to fall in love with his grandmother?" snapped Maybelle, very peevish because her idea wasn't panning out so very well.

Then a light ripped across my mind. I thought it was an inspiration.

"Maybelle," I cried out, "you're the girl! You're the girl for Jigger Bunts!"

Chapter Eighteen

Oh well, looking backward it is always easy to see where a man has made his mistakes. You can glance over the things that you did ten years ago and see where you were a fool and where you were pretty wise. And so I can see now how wild that idea was. But at the time, it looked really all right to me. I had to have a girl with looks, brains, and a sense of humor if I wanted one to handle the kid. And where could I find a better layout in all of these respects than in Maybelle Crofter Wayne, or whatever she happened to be calling herself at the time.

Maybelle looked me up and down, and then she shrugged her shoulders like a man.

"What a guy!" said Maybelle.

"What's wrong?" I asked. "Are you too proud for the job?"

"I've done a lot of stupid things, and a lot of crazy things," said Maybelle, "and I've done my share of the bad things, too. But I've never used my face and my chatter to rob the cradle. Not yet I haven't, and I'm not going to start on this baby to please you."

The idea that Maybelle herself would put any obstacles in my path made me mad. I couldn't answer for a minute, while she went on.

"The idiots that I've picked out and made simps of have always been old enough to know better. Something over thirty and something under fifty. That's my motto. I've never even soft-soaped the old baldies, or googled baby talk at 'em. Sure I'm bad. Sure I'm wicked, Tommy. But I got rules. The fight has got to be straight Marquis of Queensberry, or nothing doing."

She was funny that way. You never knew how she was coming at you. Always something unexpected. You might talk to her a hundred years, but on the last day she would flabbergast you with something that you'd never guessed about her before.

"Now look here, cutie," I said, "you can save that talk for Sunday, but every day of the week is Monday so far as I'm concerned. Don't try any of the bunk on me. I remember how you had old man Foote standing around at your door and making a fool of himself for the whole village to see when . . ."

"Hey, Tommy!" busted in Maybelle. "Leave it be, will you?"

"Sure," I said, "only when you talk proud, smile, kid, smile!"

"The old goat," sniffed Maybelle. "He was an exception, anyway, and he didn't count. You got to give a poor girl some leeway."

"Sure," I said, "and that's what I want you to take right now. All the leeway in the world, honey. I want you to start in on planning out a campaign for taming down this here young outlaw."

She shook her head.

"Listen, Maybelle . . . ," I began, but she cut me off.

"Even when you put the Y in my name, you can't persuade me on this. I'm adamant, you understand?"

"All right," I said, pretty disgusted. "You lean back in your chair and give yourself time, will you? Have a smoke."

"Yes," Maybelle said, and she takes the makings and turns out her smoke very slick and fast. I lighted it and watched her puffing and blowing rings very deliberate, as if a dozen people up and down the street weren't watching her all the time and going on to gossip about that shameless woman. But public opinion never weighed very heavy in the opinion of Maybelle Crofter.

"Now you try it in words of one syllable," I said.

"Try what?" she asked.

"Try to explain why you won't tackle this job for me?"

"Old son," Maybelle said, "you hear me talk. When I get in my work on a man like that, it isn't any joke. I don't just pop into his head and out again. I stay there for a long while. The pikers and the tin-horn sports may forget me quick enough, but the hundred percent men are different. This kid is a ham, of course. But he's a man. And suppose that he should really tumble head over heels in love with me?"

"He won't be such a fat-head," I said. "You're not such a bright light as that, Maybelle."

She just grinned at me. Then she turned the grin into a smile—which is a lot different thing, if you know what I mean. She reached out and dropped a hand on my arm and looked straight into my eyes.

"Dear old silly Tommy," she said, "don't you think that even *you* could love me if you tried a little?"

I could only blink a little. Then I shook off her hand and took a deep breath.

"Leave me be, Maybelle," I said. "I never done you no harm."

"All right," Maybelle said, "I never hit a man that's down."

I explained: "I understand what you mean. To get ahold on the kid, you've got to pretend that he's knocked your eye right out. You've got to pretend to be pretty woozy about him, and that may make him fall into something a couple of pegs deeper than calf love. But we've got to risk that. You understand what I mean? It's this or a hangman to make his future."

"Why," Maybelle said, "he seems to have been

doing pretty well for himself, thank you very much. I don't notice that he's crowding the jails much."

"You don't follow my drift," I explained to her. "Sooner or later, he'll have his back against the wall, and then when he fights, he'll have to shoot to kill. And when that happens, there'll be a slaughter. You understand, Maybelle? We got to plan on saving himself from his future."

She saw that point, at last. "All right," said Maybelle, "but what am I to do first? Ride out into the mountains and lasso this young rip?"

"Leave me to corral him," I said. "He's too much of a friend of mine not to try to drop in on me at the ranch, now that he's working this section of the country again. And when I lay hands on him, I'll try to get him interested in you."

"That's easy," said Maybelle, and she opened her purse and took out her photograph. "I pack some of these around with me all the time. You never can tell when they'll come in handy, you see? Hand the kid one of these. Wait a minute. Here's one that makes me look younger. That was last year."

You would say that she had a lot of brass, that girl. Well, she did have brass. But part of it was just frankness. She knew what her bad spots were and she was willing to confess to them. She knew what her good points were, and she was just as ready to talk about them. She was just different from other people, if you know what I mean.

I looked this photograph over. She was dressed up in a girlish-looking thing with a sailor collar on it, and a broad hat with the brim furled up a mite, like her nose.

"What deviltry were you up to when this here picture was taken last year?" I asked.

"That was when Sammy Marvin . . . no, I mean that was when Jack Roxburgh was paying attention to me. The old idiot should have married somebody forty years old, at least, but what he wanted was sweet sixteen, you see? So I thought . . . why shouldn't a man have what he wants, if it makes him happy? Anyway, it's a good picture, isn't it? My mouth doesn't look big in it."

"No," I agreed, "it doesn't. You look kind of sad and sweet?"

"That's the devil of a big mouth," says Maybelle. "You got to smile sad and sweet or else not smile at all. However, maybe the kid won't mind sadness?"

I said: "Now, you get this wrote down in red and don't you never forget it while you're on this case."

"After all, Tom Reynard," she said, "I'm a woman and not a doctor."

"You are a devil," I said, "but let's get down to business. While you're working on this kid . . ."

"Remember," Maybelle said, "I haven't got my

alimony . . . not yet."

It took me up sort of short, but I set my teeth and decided to weather it.

"I'll mail you fifty dollars to start with," I said.

"All right," Maybelle said. "It sounds like chicken feed, but beggars can't be choosers."

She didn't even blush, though she certainly knew that I was only an ordinary cowpuncher with no big pay to fall back on and not very many savings. She was a hard one, in her own way, was Maybelle.

"You mail me fifty," she said, "and then what? I start dressing like that picture . . . real girlish? Matter of fact, I'm togged out sort of young today."

"How does it happen?" I asked.

"One of my neighbors came in the other day. A sour-faced old dame. She happened to see a pretty young-looking hat lying around and she says . . . 'I really don't see, Missus Wayne, how a person of your age can wear a hat like that.' Real catty, you see? So I say . . . 'Keep your eyes open tomorrow, and you'll see for yourself.' So here I am. And not so bad at that, Tommy! Not so bad at that!"

Dog-gone me if she didn't have a little mirror out, studying herself and nodding and smiling, agreeing with herself every minute.

You couldn't beat Maybelle!

"Very well," I said. "I suppose that you might

dress young for this part you're going to play . . .
if I can ever get him to you. But look here,
Maybelle, I want you to understand that the face
won't make much difference to the kid. You got
to work by hypnosis on him. He can get blinder
than anybody in the world. So dog-goned blind
that he lived with me for weeks and still would
be thinking that I was a hero, if I hadn't turned
loose and got him out of the trance myself. That's
what you got to do. Rock him into a sweet dream,
and then everything will be easy. He'll never see
the solid earth again. He'll be miles above the
clouds."

"Well," said Maybelle, "I'll think it over. But
right offhand, it seems to me that the best thing
that I can do will be to be a wronged woman . . .
that sort of stuff usually goes over pretty big with
the youngsters."

And she let her head fall back and laughed just
as free and hearty as any man.

My, but she was a rascal, and a pretty one, too.

Chapter Nineteen

On the whole, I felt a good deal better after talking with Maybelle that way. It gave me more heart, and I went around town and did my chores. I decided that I had ought to have more chats with Maybelle before I left New Nineveh. But when I went to see her, she was away, and her neighbor to the left told me without being asked that young Mrs. Wayne had gone gadding off with a strange man that afternoon.

I don't know why it is that good women hate the bad ones so much. I don't pretend to be any great judge, you understand, but it does always seem to me that their malice has a shading of envy in it. However, I ask the pardon of every lady for saying a thing like that.

Anyway, I knew as I went back down the street that it wouldn't be the fault of the other women in the town if the admirers of Maybelle didn't learn too much about her for her own good. When I got to the hotel again, I intended to start right back for the ranch, but I didn't.

There was a man blew in from Montana that said he owned most of the silver mines in that part of the world, and besides that he said that he had corralled about all the luck that there was, and he added that in his spare time he had invented a little game with cards, by the name of poker.

I allowed that I had heard of that game and would like to learn a little more about it. Three more of the boys of New Nineveh said that they were always willing to learn, and so we all sat in, smiling at each other as he "taught" us. Dog-gone me if he didn't know every trick there was. There was a time that night when my watch and my hunting knife and my Colt were all lying on top of that table. But after a while I got them back into my pockets, and then luck turned my way a little. Particular when I suggested that we hire a gent for a dealer, because after that the gent from Montana wasn't so dog-goned sure about his invention, and his silver mines didn't seem to be worth half so much.

Anyway, about two o'clock we got him parted from the last of his wad, and, though only about thirty dollars come to my share, it looked pretty fair to me for one day's work.

I went up to my room singing, with the gents that I waked up on the way cussing me hearty on either side of the hall. But when I opened the door and stepped into my room, the first thing that I seen was a shadow against the stars beyond my window. That was nothing much to make a fuss over, I agree, but this shadow happened to wear the shape of a man.

"Who is it?" I said, but I was so scared that my

voice wasn't any louder than a whisper. I looked closer and I could see that his head was lying on his arms where he sat at my table, and then I could hear the breathing of the sleeper.

Of course, I just thought that it was some drunk who had got into the wrong room and had fallen asleep before he could get into bed. I lighted a match, but the minute that the flame flared, I dropped that match and stepped on it, for fear somebody else might see what I was looking at.

Because the face that was turned sideways toward me on those folded arms was the face of the bandit, the outlaw, the stick-up artist that the whole range was howling to get at, and New Nineveh was howling the loudest of all. It was Jigger Bunts.

"Jigger!" I gasped at his ear.

He woke up and stretched and yawned. Then he jumped up and shook hands with me and started saying how glad he was to see me again.

"Except that I'm *not* seeing you!" said Jigger. And he scratched a match and lighted a lamp. It drove me wild.

"Suppose that someone looks in?" I said.

"Not much chance of that," he said. "It's a pretty far climb to get up to that window. I know, because I've tried it myself, this evening."

"But if they catch you here, they've got you trapped and helpless, sure."

"Maybe not," said Jigger.

"What could you do, if they get under that window, and watched you there?"

"I might try to force the back door, or rush right out the front way. Or I might go up to the top of the house and jump for the next roof . . . that's not more than fifteen feet away, you know."

Fifteen feet across a regular ravine, with hard rocks underneath if you missed your foothold on the far side.

"Do you even know how to get onto the roof?" I asked.

"Oh, yes," said the kid. "I haven't overlooked all the lessons that you gave me about Louis Dalfieri, you know!"

"What lessons?" I asked.

"You remember telling me how Dalfieri never went anyplace without looking over the ways of escape. I haven't forgotten that, and when I found that you weren't in your room here, I looked the hotel over to get acquainted with it."

"How did you know that I was here?" I barked at him.

"I stuck up a farmer driving a buckboard out of town and I was asking him about what had been happening in town. He told me pretty freely. The idiot seemed to have an idea that I'd murder him at the first slip he made. Good heavens, Reynard, Louis Dalfieri never gave an impression like that, did he? He never seemed such a blood-curdling ruffian."

155

How was I to remember exactly the colors in which all of us in the bunkhouse had painted the picture of Louis Dalfieri in the old days, those long months and months before?

I admitted that I suppose Dalfieri would not.

"But you held up a fighting man for the sake of getting news out of him?" I asked the kid, sort of sick and weak.

"He wasn't a fighting man," he said.

"They all pack guns . . . they all can use them . . . these gents in New Nineveh," I told him. "And it's time for you to know that, if you haven't gathered it already."

He only shook his head before replying.

"There's a difference between a dangerous man and a weak one," said Jigger Bunts. "You can tell them by something in their eyes . . . the way that they look at you and the way that they carry their heads. Dalfieri could always tell the bad ones . . . you remember, Tom?"

Dalfieri again, damn the brain that invented him!

He went on: "I heard about the poker game you were sitting in on. And then that you were staying at the hotel. So I came in after dark and drifted through the rooms until I found the one that had your things in it. It was like seeing a friend's face when I laid eyes on them, Tom."

And he laid a hand on my shoulder and smiled at me. But all I could think of was the incredible daring of this young fool, wandering from room to room in a hotel where he might run into danger at any time, and where every exit could be barred against him in no time.

"Then you sat down and went to sleep," I said.

"Well," Jigger began, "you see there was only about one chance in five that anybody would come into the room before you did. I needed sleep . . . haven't had any in two days. And you remember what Dalfieri used to say about chances?"

"Damn Dalfieri!" I said.

He was shocked. Plain shocked and staggered by hearing language that was a sort of a blasphemy to him.

He said with a crooked smile: "Of course, that's a joke, but it doesn't sound like a good joke to me, Tom, if you'll let me say so. However, you remember that Dalfieri says that four chances out of five is as good as a sure thing . . . to a man who's living in danger of the law. So I had to take it. And I've won out, you see? I've had . . . let me see . . . why, four whole hours of sleep. It bucks me up no end."

He straightened himself a little and shook back his shoulders. You would never say that that young dandy had gone forty-eight hours without sleep. He was the thing that Louis Dalfieri, the moving-picture actor, had tried to be like, but had missed out on.

Everything was perfect. And the Lord knows how much it would have cost a man to go right into a store and try to buy all that stuff. He had the flowing tie of black silk under his chin, and he wore a silk shirt with gold buttons, big gold buttons on it. Queer-looking buttons they were, but when I looked closer I could recognize them. Now and then a very flashy Mexican *caballero* will put a little plate of gold, like a coin, on the peak of his sombrero. And that was what the seven buttons of Jigger Bunts's shirt were.

I wondered how Jigger had got those seven little plates that had once finished off the gaudy sombreros of seven bucks. I could make a guess that he hadn't bought them in any curio shop. Because Jigger was not that kind of a man. For instance, Dalfieri in the picture had a sash around his waist. And now so did Jigger Bunts. But the sash of Jigger was made of thin yellow Chinese silk all brocaded with fine gold figurings that hardly showed. They looked like little metal casings. Lord knows what that wonderful scarf had been intended for originally by the hands that had put in the years at this embroidery—an altar cloth, perhaps.

No, nothing was too good in the line of clothes once Jigger started to dress for the part of Louis Dalfieri, the outlaw that probably never rode a horse outside of the bunkhouse where the boys and I invented him! From his shining boots to his neat little waxed and pointed mustaches, Jigger looked like something off the stage, not like a real, hundred percent bandit. Poor kid!

He said: "Tom, you look down-hearted. What's wrong?"

"Forget me, Jigger," I said, "and tell me about yourself."

A shadow came across his eyes.

"I haven't found him yet," said Jigger. "I've ridden hundreds of miles on horseback, and I've ridden thousands of miles on the blind baggage or the rods or on top of boxcars. I've pried into every nook and cranny that I could find, but I haven't found Dalfieri."

Maybe some people would have laughed. But I felt just the other way. It was no laughing matter when this kid set his fool heart on something.

"And what's strangest of all," Jigger said, "is that I haven't found anyone who knows about him. Of course, I remember you always said that he worked very quietly. Not very many men knew him. Still, it seems odd . . . mighty odd!"

I hoped, for a minute, that the truth might be dawning in that brain of his—or the first doubt, at least. And if there was just the beginning of a doubt, then I could confess the whole hoax that we had played on him, though of course it would make him loathe me like a snake.

He said: "But what a man he is, Tom! To do the things that he's done, and yet to keep so quiet that not one man in ten thousand ever heard of his name. Why, when I think of him, I have to take off my hat. I have to do it!"

And he did! He took off his hat and stood there with his head back, and the long, shining black hair curling almost down to his shoulders. He was like something out of a storybook. A fairytale, not a fact!

No, I could see that the wonder might be growing in him, but there was no doubt as yet. And if I started in cold blood to tell about the lie we had worked on him, he simply wouldn't believe me. The time hadn't come when I could do that part of my duty for him.

So I had to try the other string in my bow. I had to fall back on Maybelle Crofter.

"Well, old-timer," I said, "I'll tell you what's making me blue. And it's a thing where I need help."

"Ah, Tom," he said, "if I could do a good turn for you, it would be the happiest day in my life!"

Chapter Twenty

He meant it, too. He was as deceiving and mysterious as a good pane of polished glass. He was as subtle as a bull buffalo and as hard to outguess as a hen in a chicken yard. He stood up there with his face shining at me and his eyes snapping. He wanted me to tell him to fight ten men, or find a gold mine, or hold up an express train single-handed, or do something else man-sized like that. But it would've made you laugh to see his face fall when I said to him that my trouble had to do with the affairs of a woman!

He lost interest right away and began to smile down at me in a very superior sort of way, as though I was to be pitied and wondered at for wasting my time on anything as lowdown and useless as a woman.

He said in an easy way: "You're fallen in love with some girl, I suppose, Tom."

"Yes," I said, "I have."

"Just lately, then?" the kid asked.

I thought about that. "No," I said, "it's been about four years since I first fell in love with her."

That was not a complete lie. In a way, I had been half in love with pretty Maybelle Crofter from the time that she got out of childhood. She had such looks and such ways about her.

Anyway, this speech made a terrible hit with the kid.

He stepped back.

"Tom," he said under his breath, "you don't mean that you have loved a woman for years . . . not saying a word about it ever . . . My God, Tom, but you're a wonderful man!"

Yes, sir, the raving young idiot was going to start in worshipping me again. I never saw a boy like that. He was positively miserable unless he found somebody to make a hero out of.

"You see, old-timer," I had to put in, "it's this way . . . she was only a kid when I first knew her."

"Don't explain to me," said the kid. "It's like something out of an old romance . . . like the way the knights used to love their ladies in the old times. Here you are, and me knowing you so long and so well, but I never guessed it. Never dreamed that you ever so much as *thought* of a woman!"

There he was at it. He was always reading some sort of rot in books that he picked up, and then trying to apply what he read about knights in armor to real cowpunchers in chaps and bandannas.

I only shook my head. I didn't know exactly what to say next.

"But tell me," the kid said, very excited, "why you're so sad, Tom? Won't she have you?"

"She won't," I confirmed. "And she can't. She's married!"

"Heavens!" the kid blurts out. "Heavens, old man!"

He goes over and leans at the window with tears in his eyes. Yes, I mean what I say! There was tears in his eyes! He was actually standing there and suffering for me. There was a frown on his face, he was working so hard to keep from showing his emotion.

He says, deep and quiet: "I always knew that there was a secret sorrow in your life, chief. I always guessed it when I sat and watched you when you were silent."

That was typical. Seeing me when I was too tired to talk, he turned my ache in the shoulders into an ache of the heart.

"Never mind that," I said. "What matters now is . . ."

"I've got to mind that!" the kid sings out, so excited that I was afraid that somebody close by my room might hear him through the tissue-paper walls of that crazy old shack of a hotel. "I've got to mind," he says, "how you've swallowed your troubles, and never winced! Why, chief, when I look at you and think what kind of a man you are, it makes me feel like . . . like a fool and a baby. I tell you, chief, that it makes me put you up there with . . . with Louis Dalfieri himself!"

He got rid of the tears that were in his eyes—

tears of sympathy for my grief. He got a new set. Tears of joy because I was so wonderful and so great and so grand, and because he could have the pleasure of looking at me with his own eyes. And he could stand there in the same room with me and breathe the same air.

Oh, damn such a boy as he was!

"Jigger," I said, "is this a time to think about me or about Louis Dalfieri, even? It's a time to talk about that poor girl!"

"Ah," the kid said, "I thought that your trouble was just because you never could marry her, chief. But I see, now, you wouldn't trouble yourself about such things. You wouldn't ask help for yourself. It's because you want to help her out of some sort of trouble."

He was busy putting some more gilding on my wings.

"Son," I said, "I can't tell you what it would mean to me if I could help this poor girl."

"Tom, Tom!" he said. "Could you use me? Could you please let me try to be of help to you or to her?"

"It's no good, Jigger," I told him. "It ain't any good. You ain't the sort of a man who could help a woman like her."

He was humble enough, but he had his pride, and now he bit his lip. And then he sings out: "I want to do what I can, partner, if you'll only tell me what it is that I can do!"

"Nothing, Jigger," I tell him, very sad. "I see that there's nothing that you can do. You could never settle down and live quietly, keeping out of the sight of folks."

"Why couldn't I?" Jigger asked, getting excited. "Would you please tell me why I couldn't be quiet?"

"Oh, I know you, Jigger," I replied. "Pretty near as well as I know myself. Yes, maybe better, even. What you want to do is to be out there in the hills, galloping along and living wild and free and fine, the same way as Dalfieri himself and the rest of them great wild men have lived. It would be poison to you to settle down and be quiet . . ."

"You don't know me, chief," he said, fairly stuttering with eagerness. "Dog-gone it, I tell you that you don't know me. Gallop around over the hills? Live wild and free? Why, chief, do you think that it's any pleasure to me to be herded around the mountains like a wolf? No, only it's my fate to be an outcast hounded by enemies, surrounded by hate . . ."

He stopped for a minute. There were such tears of self-pity in his eyes that he couldn't go on for a while. He had kidded himself into a great state of mind. He was all worked up. When he got that way, sometimes he would open up and talk like sixty. He would talk as good as you could find in a book. And mostly his speeches used to come out of some of the yarns that he used to read, I think.

I had to bite my tongue to keep from laughing in his face, and I said: "You don't really mean it, Jigger. You don't really mean that it's distasteful to you, living high and free and wild, the way that you do?"

"No," the kid admitted. "Living doomed and desolate though I do, my secret yearning is for some quiet corner of the world . . . a house of peace, and a little garden where I could work with hoe and spade . . ."

Here he got so choked with sorrow for himself that he had to stop again and let off steam. The idea of him ever turning his hand to a cottage and a hoe made me smile inside—but, after all, anything was possible for that kid, if the right sort of suggestion was used on him.

"I see how it is," I said, keeping my face fairly straight. "And it gives me a lot more hope that maybe you *could* help her. Except that it would be terribly hard. Mind you, I would try the job myself, but she wouldn't let me. She wouldn't let me sacrifice myself for her. She's that fine, Jigger. She would do some terrible wild thing if she thought that she was messing up my life!"

Jigger blinked and swallowed the idea on the wing, so to speak.

"I see," he said, "that she must be a wonderful woman."

"She is," I agreed, "different from any woman that I ever met or that I ever heard of."

Which was exactly the truth, as you'll agree with me before you've heard the finish about Maybelle.

"But," I said, "to take care of her you would have to actually take the terrible danger of finding a way of living right here in the middle of this here town. The idea of a horrible risk like that . . . why it makes me sick to think of it even. It would mean living, say, in the barn behind her house, and keeping yourself out of the sight of everybody as long as the sun was shining and only sneaking out at night . . . like a wild tiger right in the middle of the town . . ."

Terrible? I could see that Jigger Bunts was almost swooning with happiness to think of tackling such a job.

"Chief," he said, "even if it's dangerous, I would like to give it a try."

I raised my hand.

"Don't tell me about it," I warned. "Because the more that I think about it, the more I see that it would be sort of suicide for you to attempt it. Too many men are out gunning for you. And if they saw you . . . well, you might get away, but that would be an end of the protection that poor . . . I can't tell her name, though."

"Chief," gasped the kid, "I beg you to tell me."

"No, no," I told him. "I wouldn't dream of it.

Why, youngster, this here is a harder thing than I've ever heard of before. Not you nor any man could ever do it."

He was foaming, now, with despair and enthusiasm.

He said: "Tom, I want to beg a little favor of you."

"Jigger," I said, pretending not to understand, "of course I would do anything that I could for you."

He said: "Tell me the name of the girl."

"It's not fair, trapping me like that," I told him. "But I suppose that I've got to live up to my promise to you. Her name is Maybelle Wayne."

"Chief," he said, "if you won't send me to her, I'll go myself and offer myself to guard her."

I swallowed a smile again.

"Jigger," I told him, "I like your nerve, I got to admit. But before you ring into this game, you've got to know what you're to guard her from."

"Aye," he agrees. "That's it."

"I . . . you'll have to ask her yourself," I let him know. "And let her tell you in her own words . . . what the danger is, because I can't do it half so well. And here, Jigger, is a picture of her."

I had held back that photograph for the last minute, and now I passed it across to Jigger Bunts.

Well, he wasn't of age, and until a man gets along toward thirty he has a weakness for girlishness, and again after he's fifty. The only period when he's fairly safe is between thirty and fifty. Jigger had never paid much attention to girls. He'd been much too busy finding himself heroes, of one kind and another, and getting himself ready to imitate them. The amount of hours he had sunk in studying in the dress of Louis Dalfieri for instance would've made him a pretty good actor on the stage. And as for the time that he had invested in fancy shooting—why, I would hate to guess at it, but I know from what he told me, that he spent five hours a day for six weeks in practicing a quick whirl around and a shot from the hip.

So you can see how it was that Maybelle could step in his mind without any competition to give her a run for her money. I sized the situation up for a while, watching poor young Jigger simply turn groggy with wonder as he stared at that snapshot.

Then I said: "I'm going to keep you right here in this room until tomorrow night. And then I'm going to take you to see Maybelle."

Chapter Twenty-One

Keeping Jigger inside four walls was like keeping a royal Bengal tiger in a hen house. He was wanting to rip loose, every minute. He was always pretending humility and gentleness. But the fighting devil that had always been pretty strong in that youngster had been given a pretty thorough cultivating during the past months when he was free to roam up and down the range as he would.

I had to watch him like a hawk all the time that he was with me, and in the middle of the next afternoon, I made him swear not to budge out of the room while I was gone—then I started for Maybelle.

She had a house on the edge of town that her husband had fixed up for her after he decided that he couldn't leave her with his folks on their ranch. And when l sauntered up to her door, the piano was rattling and Maybelle's voice was chirping out a rag tune.

When she came to the door and found me there, she brought me right in and introduced me to a tall young chap with a brown face that was never got except prospecting or punching cows. He'd come into money lately. And the coin was busting out like a rash all over him. He had an emerald stickpin that looked like a big green eye in the middle of his red necktie. And he had a wallet that looked like a football in the throat of an ostrich. I forget what his name was.

She sashayed into the room and said: "Here's my lawyer come to talk business to me, dearie. You run along, and don't stand on the corner with your hat off because there's sunstroke in the air. So long!"

The big guy backed out the door and gave me a dangerous look while he was passing out.

"You're kind of rough on that gent," I said to Maybelle. "He knows that I'm no lawyer."

"What difference does it make, foolish?" Maybelle said. "He's the kind that likes to be handled rough. Anything to get him out of his trance. He's had a rush of dollars to the head and he can't think straight. Now sit down and tell me about Jigger Bunts. I've been dreaming about him in the middle of the day."

"That's because he's coming to see you tonight," I told her.

She was a good deal surprised by that, and so I went ahead and told her when Jigger had showed up, and how.

"Just crazy!" said Maybelle. "But what'll I tell him is the danger, when you bring him around tonight? I'm in no danger from anything."

"You work that up yourself," I said. "If this is a partnership job, Maybelle, I've done more than

171

fifty percent, already. Now you do your part. The thing for you to do is to look young and get a pair of wings. He says he can see already that you're one of the most wonderful women in the world. He won't see much of you. Just his idea of you."

"I've to prune down the slang," Maybelle commented. "Talking English is a terrible strain. Does the poor fish have to live in my barn while he protects me from things that ain't?"

"It's the only way," I explained to her. "I've got him all heated up about the idea. Now, Maybelle, when you get that young man out there in the barn, the thing for you to do is to imagine that you got a wild hawk in your hand. You got to teach him to come when you whistle. You got to get him tamed. And when it comes to working out the saving of him, we'll do that together. Main thing for you is to keep him put safe. If he keeps on rampaging around, sticking up stages and whatnot, he'll be ripening himself for the gallows in no time."

She agreed that that was the thing to do.

I had a couple of other people to see, and it was already the warm evening of the day, and the town was settling down—as much as New Nineveh ever settled down—when I started back for the hotel. The sprinklers were whizzing and swishing on the front lawns of the houses that I passed, and the householders were out in their shirt sleeves, hollering their opinions about

172

weather and politics to each other. Everything was peaceful until I got pretty close to the hotel, and then there was a sudden yipping of men, half scared and half mad, and the barking of Colts, deep and hoarse.

When I come around the corner, keeping close to the building, I saw half a dozen gents in the vacant lot next to the hotel, ripping around and shooting at shadows.

"Where did he go?" they were yelling.

"He went behind that tree."

"No, he started straight back for the hotel."

"You lie! He ducked out on the street."

"He headed for behind the blacksmith shop."

I hung around until they had quieted down a mite, and then I found out what had been happening. The deputy sheriff, Hendon, had been just standing there talking to some of the boys. Telling them that they had got to quiet down because he was gonna bring law and order into that town of New Nineveh if he had to kill himself doing it. And the boys agreed that it was time for the old town to turn over a new page, but they suggested that the first thing for him to do was to get out on the trail and run down Jigger Bunts.

The deputy sheriff agreed that that was a fine idea, but he said that he had already worked himself ragged on the trail of Jigger Bunts after the stage hold-up, but that all he could figure out was that Bunts had headed right straight back for New Nineveh itself, and when he came to that point, he decided to give up the search altogether, for the time being. Because, as he pointed out, it was madness to imagine that even Jigger Bunts would dare to try to hide himself in New Nineveh.

He said that he would get Jigger before long, though, and he said that the chief trouble with the other folks who had ridden out to get him was that they were licked and ready to be bluffed out before they ever got within shooting distance of the kid. But he, Hendon, wasn't going to be bluffed.

It was the blacksmith that told me this stuff, talking behind his hand. He was a hard one, that blacksmith, but he didn't want his opinions to get aired.

"They got about that far in their yarning, and the boys was beginning to agree to everything that this here Hendon said," the blacksmith informed me, "when dog-gone me if a shadow didn't drop out of the branches of that fir tree, yonder, and right into the bunch of them. And it started a flock of trouble, because that shadow had the action of a wildcat and the shape of a man. It landed right on poor Hendon, first of all, and squashed his hat. And then it flickered around for about ten seconds, and everything that it touched went flat. Just about the time that the guns began to chatter, the shadow disappeared, and the boys have been milling around ever since, trying to locate it."

Now, before that story was half told, a chilly idea had begun to percolate into my brain and send a shiver clean down the length of my spine. I said to the blacksmith: "Who could it have been? Some drunk having a party all by himself?"

"Drunk?" said the blacksmith, grinning sidewise at me. "Well, no drunk that I've ever seen was half as fast on his feet or hit half as hard with his fists. But my idea is that the shadow that dropped on those boobs and flattened them out was Jigger Bunts!"

It was my idea, too, of course.

I separated myself from the blacksmith as soon as I could and I slid into the hotel and up to my room. The whole town was beginning to wake up all over again, and men were hunting everywhere for the fellow that had played the joke on the deputy sheriff and his gang of pals. Except that most of the people that I met in the lobby of the hotel swore that the shadow must have been wearing brass knuckles.

Well, I knew something about the strength in the hands and the shoulders of Jigger, and there was something so foolish and childish and useless about the whole proceeding that I could have sworn that it was Jigger and nobody else.

When I got up to the room, whatever doubts I

had were put to rest. Because there I found Jigger walking up and down with a long, soft, easy stride, like a walking cat when it figures that a mouse is probably behind the next door.

When I popped in, Jigger whirled around on me as though he expected that I might be the mouse. The lamp wasn't lighted. I could hardly see him, but his satisfaction sort of lighted up the room for me. He was as happy as a kid with a whole Christmas tree to himself.

"I thought you'd be having a sleep, Jigger," I said. "Or cleaning your guns, or something like that."

"I slept myself out," said Jigger, "and I'd finished cleaning my guns . . . when I decided that a little air wouldn't do me any harm. So I just went out for a little walk."

"Jigger," I said, "you swore to me that you wouldn't leave this room until I got back to it, didn't you?"

It knocked him all in a heap, as the saying is.

"Old-timer," he answers, "I'm terribly sorry. I just forgot all about it."

"Maybe you'll explain how come that you forgot," I snapped, pretty stern, "and maybe you'll explain, too, what all of this shooting has been about? And finally, maybe you'll tell me how a gent that acts the way that you've been doing the first day that you're put on your good behavior, is going to be able to play soft and low and take care of a poor lonely girl like . . . ?"

He was repentant. He fairly crawled to get back into my good opinion. He said that as he sat at the window, he could hear them talking. And it was a little irritating to him. He didn't intend to make any trouble. But he wanted to see them closer, and so he leaned out of the window and eased himself into the big fir tree that stood next to the wall—and after that—well, the temptation was too great.

I went to the window and looked out. The tip of the nearest branch of that tree was six feet away. How could anything but a bird or a monkey get into the tree at that distance.

Well, I don't know to this day!

Chapter Twenty-Two

I waited about half an hour, and during that time some of the furor died away in the town. They were still hunting for the stranger who had broken up Hendon's little party, but they weren't hunting with half so much vim when I said to Jigger: "Now, son, I'm going to go down to the street and turn up to the right. In about five minutes, I'll be at the second corner, and I'll wait there for a minute or two. After that, I'll expect that you'll be watching and following me, though how you'll get there, I leave to you."

That didn't seem to upset him at all. I went down into the lobby and there I found big Hendon. He was a mess. There was a big cut under one eye and his nose looked like a red balloon moored to his face and about ready to rise. He was pretty hot, and he was telling the men down there that he was sure that the man who had done these things to him had gotten into the hotel. Hendon intended to search the place. In the meantime, he told what a cowardly thing it had been—for a man to drop out of a tree on top of him!

Nobody dared to smile, because Hendon was a known man. But I went out onto the street, and heard a fellow in a corner of the room saying softly: "It looks more like the work of Bunts than of any other man I know."

It looked like Jigger Bunts to them and that was the reason that New Nineveh was so worked up over a mere fistfight. For that town hated Jigger Bunts as I've said before. The very fact that he was so decent in his very crimes was a thing that made the town hate him more than ever. And there were a full twenty real badmen in New Nineveh. The history of the town read like a few pages out of a jail record. But if New Nineveh had never done any other thing, it had always made itself respected as a fighting community—and yet here was a fellow who came along and made a mock of them and started to work first on the outskirts of the town with a stage hold-up—and then came in and beat up their leading citizens with his bare hands—half a dozen of them at a time!

No wonder New Nineveh was angry. Any other town might have been, for a smaller provocation than this!

When I got to the second street crossing, I waited for a minute, making a cigarette, and then I went slowly on again. When I came to the house of Maybelle Wayne, I stood again just inside of the big hedge that circled the yard. There wasn't a sound from the house. And its face was black, except for a single lighted window on the first floor. The smell of the wet lawn and the sound of the sprinkler that was still spinning with a hushing murmur in a distant corner of the yard made me feel like I had come back to a real home.

It was Maybelle's work, of course. She knew how to play a part. And if she had to turn a whole house and lot into part of her stage, why, she could do it!

There was a soft, cat-like step crossing the sidewalk, and here was Jigger Bunts beside me.

"Sorry I'm late," he whispered. "But a fellow saw me down the street and started to hold me up . . ."

"Good God, Jigger, what did you do?"

"It wouldn't do to have any noise. I knew that that might spoil everything. Besides, I knew that you were pretty mad at me because I'd . . . er . . . had a little party earlier in the evening. So I tied this chap up and left him there with a gag between his teeth. I'm terribly sorry that I'm late."

That was like Jigger. He took himself and his ways for granted. He was the only living human being that could!

I took him up to the front door, but he wasn't in any rush. He kept whispering: "Wait a minute, Tom. I want you to brush me off. I'm pretty dusty. This necktie doesn't hang any too well . . . a man like Dalfieri . . . why, he'd never appear any place looking so rough as I do now."

Dalfieri, Dalfieri, Dalfieri! How damned tired I was of that name.

After I had knocked at the front door, there was no answer, except that the light went out in the front room.

The kid grabbed me by the shoulder. "Look," he whispered. "You've frightened her."

"Go on," I said. "What's there to frighten her in a knock at her front door?" I rapped again.

After a while, there was a rustle in the hall, and then as I knocked a third time, the door was pulled open about a quarter of an inch.

"Who is there?" said a whisper, very shaky.

"Tom Reynard," I answered, swallowing a grin.

She was slick, was Maybelle, but I never imagined that she would stack the cards like this.

When she heard my voice and name, she jerked the door open wide.

"Oh," Maybelle gasped, "a friend!"

She was revealed, as they say in the papers, all dressed up in white, with her hands clasped at her breast, breathing hard and fast.

"Were you scared, Maybelle?" I asked.

"Oh, Tom . . . dear Tom," she said. "Thank God that it is only you . . . I thought . . . I thought no . . . no, I can't say it!"

The little cat! She was going it a bit strong. I was afraid that even the kid would begin to see through this.

I said: "I've brought a friend to see you, Maybelle."

"A friend of yours, Tom," she responded, "will be my friend, too, I trust and pray."

Dog-gone her, where did she pick up words like that? Just plain book talk, near as bad as Jigger Bunts's own kind.

"But I must get a light," she announced. "When I first heard you come, I thought that the lamp might give an enemy light to . . ." She left that unfinished and went scuttling off down the hall with her dress whispering around her.

The kid grabbed me by the shoulder. "Oh God, Tom," he whispered, "how terrible. Who would think it? A woman afraid of what men may do to her . . . afraid . . . that they'll see her. Oh, I'd like to do ten murders on the strength of this."

"Leave go of my arm!" I snapped at him. "Leave go of me before your fingers scrape the bone. Maybe you will do ten murders before you're through with it!"

She got a lamp lighted and came out into the black hall and held the lamp up above her head so we could see our way—and see her, too.

She was worth seeing, I got to admit.

She was all dressed up in white, skimpy and slender. She had no color on her except a red rosebud with its whole green stem pinned across her breast, diagonal. She had that yellow hair of hers done into a pigtail that snaked down her back, and the lamplight flared and fluttered and sparkled on it, and turned it into gold.

I have always figured that there is as much in the way that a pretty woman holds herself as there is in her beauty alone. If a girl has a beautiful face, she's got to have a beautiful way, too, or else she'll never show it off. She's got to learn to stand up in the eye of the world as much as to say: "Here I come. Now is your chance for a good look at me, boys. Don't miss me, because I'm worth seeing!"

I mean, they don't have to be artful other ways. But I've seen fourteen-year-old girls—yes, and little kids hardly more than able to toddle— that had that same air. They know that there is something dog-goned neat about them, and they want the world to stand off and take a good look at them.

Well, I hardly need to say that Maybelle had this air. She kept it in her pocket most of the time, but tonight she had taken it out and she wore it like a light in her face. I hardly looked at her. I kept my eye fixed on the kid, and dog-gone me if it wasn't almost sad, he was so hard hit. He stood there in his waxed-up mustache and his wild reputation, and he gaped at her as though she had been a fairy, and he a five-year-old kid.

She led us into the living room, and I had to support the kid. He was so weak and shaken that he was trembling. I don't think he could have budged from the spot where she first hit him like a thunderbolt.

I pressed a mite ahead of him, and I said quietly to Maybelle: "Loosen up a mite, will you? You've got him paralyzed."

Well, she turns around, with one of her hands resting on the table in the light of the lamp. Usually, she was pretty brown, because she loved the outdoors, and she wasn't particular about a hat. That was how come that the sun had faded a good deal of the gold out of her hair. But tonight, she had put the gold right back into that hair, and she had gummed up her hands and face and neck with powder so that they looked crystal white—but not a bit floury, the way that some girls do themselves.

She sure looked shrinking and delicate and so dog-goned tender that she would melt in your mouth, so to speak.

"Maybelle," I said, "I want you to know my friend Jerry Burns. Jerry, this is Maybelle Wayne."

Of course, I couldn't right out and introduce him by his outlawed name.

But what did Maybelle do? When I spoke her married name, she caught up both hands quick to her face and she stood there sort of swaying for a minute at the side of the table.

"Oh, Tom! Oh, Tom!" she cried with a break in her voice. "Do I have to take that name even to your friends?"

When she covered up her face and registered

pain, the kid reached her in one jump. He didn't know what to do. He wanted to help her. He wanted to support her. He wanted to show her that names didn't make any difference to him. He wanted to make it clear to her that even if her name was mud it wouldn't keep him from knowing how beautiful and clean and good and wonderful she was!

He stood about, first on one foot and then on the other, like the worst young jackass in the world.

And then he would look at me, as much as to say: "Tell me what to do! Tell me what to do!"

I didn't know myself. I only leaned close to Maybelle and whispered: "You're laying this stuff on pretty thick."

She whispers right back: "The poor kid is eating it up. Don't tell me what to do. I know him like I was his mammy."

Then she looks up and puts down her hands, and her eyes they were all teary and bright and sad, and her lips were trembling, and her head was a little to one side, and she went up and held out her hand toward him a little ways, like she was afraid that maybe she wasn't good enough to shake hands with him.

She said: "I don't know that you can wish to . . . wish to . . ."

She was choked, she was.

What did the kid do? Oh, he done something

out of a book, of course, because it was a lot too good an opportunity for him to miss. He drops on one knee and takes her hand in his and raises it to his lips.

It nearly floored me. Maybelle, she was as cool as marble, and there were no nerves added when the stuff that she was made of was first mixed up. But even Maybelle was a little staggered by this. She blinked, and she said to me with her lips: "Good Gawd, Tom, what sort of a fish is this?"

Right on top of that, she had to look down and catch her hand away from him and stand back and be all confused and startled and embarrassed, and she done it fine, and the kid got up and looked like the "Boy on the Burning Deck" in that poem.

Well, it was just sickening. It's like a moving-picture close-up. I couldn't stand it. I stood back behind the kid and made a face at Maybelle.

She only gives me a horrible sugar-and-water smile and she said: "Dear Tom, how kind and good you are to me. Have you brought another friend into my life?"

Chapter Twenty-Three

I suppose that she had a right to do the job in her own way, but, all the same, it was pretty hard on me, as you can see for yourself. I stood it as well as I could, but then I said to Maybelle: "I want you and Bunts to have a chance for a good talk. I'll go out on the verandah in front . . . and watch in the dark."

I said it real dangerous.

"Oh," Maybelle said, "you always think of everything."

And she ran along with me, real girlish, toward the door, saying: "You big fish, are you gonna leave me here with this tub of cold water? While you sit outside and listen? You'll have bad dreams for this, Tom Reynard!"

Well, sir, I was so glad to be shut of that room and all of the foolery that was going on inside of it that I hardly knew what to do. And then I walked up and down the front lawn for the length of time that it took me to smoke one cigarette.

Then I heard the piano begin, very soft and light, and what do you think that she was playing? Some go-get-'em tune like she knew how to reel out? No, sir, I tell you that what that little devil was singing was "The Last Rose of Summer," so dog-goned sad and pathetic that it pretty near choked me—and not just with laughing, either! Well, after I had finished my cigarette, I walked up onto the verandah to see how the show was coming along, and what did I see?

There was the kid sitting at the table with his face dropped in both hands, and yonder was Maybelle Crofter leaning back in the couch, wringing her hands a good deal, and keeping her eyes closed and her brows lifted, real cinematic.

Now and then the kid jerked up his head and grabbed his heart and gave himself a look at her, and that would knock him all in a heap again, and he would start in again and hold his head.

It was pretty ridiculous. And yet I had to admire Maybelle. I had been wondering how she would cover up her slangy talk and her slangy way, but when I seen her that evening, she was pure Hollywood and nothing else at all.

Suddenly the kid jumped up. He was facing the window direct, and so I could tell pretty clear what he said, which was: "Don't tell me any more. I don't want to hear. It just makes me sick!"

He looked like it did, too. But she went on.

"I want you to know. It . . . it would kill me to have you as a friend unless you knew all the terrible truth about me. And . . . and . . . you must know that I have been married three times."

"Three times!" cried the kid, turning simply white.

I got a little pale myself. It looked to me as though Maybelle had chucked her cards right out through the window and thrown away a fine winning game.

She continued: "Yes. The first time was because my poor father was growing weak with sickness . . ."

I remembered old Crofter. That old tough devil never had a sick day in his life, unless you was to count the heartaches that his daughter give him.

"And I found a man who wanted to marry me . . . who promised to give my poor father everything that . . ."

"No, no!" yelled the kid.

Maybelle bowed her head.

"You didn't!" the kid said.

"I married him," she responded.

The kid, he locks his hands above his head and went through the room in one or two strides, very grand, and he turned around and come back through it again.

It struck me sort of queer. Here were two fakers. Only, one of them was unconscious and didn't know that he was faking. But the girl, she was just on a stage, and having a wonderful good time out of it.

"And then . . . I discovered that he . . . that he didn't keep all his promises, Mister Burns."

"The lying, cowardly, traitorous sneak!" the kid hissed.

Yes, he meant it well enough, and while he paced up and down the room, Maybelle turned her head toward the window and shakes it at me, pretty thoughtful, as much as to say: "This kid is nitroglycerine, and I don't want him to explode!"

"And then . . . after he was gone . . ."

"Dead?" whispered the kid gloomily.

"Divorced," Maybelle answered, very resigned.

"Ah," the kid said. "He is still living . . . and then . . . ?"

You could see what he meant. It was written all over his face in letters a mile high. When he got the first chance, he would turn that divorced man into a divorced corpse.

"And then," went on Maybelle, "I was left alone. My father was dead. My husband was gone . . ."

"And no alimony for you?" the kid barked.

I was surprised that he knew as much as that even, and Maybelle seemed a little taken aback, too.

She said: "Oh, Mister Burns, do you think that I could take money . . . or even a crust of bread . . . from a man that I didn't love?"

Confound her, how did she dare to say such lies as that, when all the kid had to ask her was—where did she get the house and the clothes that she was living in right at that minute? But of course, no question as low and common and full of sense as that would ever come into the kid's brain. You could depend upon him being solid bone from the ears up.

He was smashed all to bits, you might say, for having seemed to suspect that she could do anything as low and terrible indecent as take alimony from a divorced husband.

I happened to remember that divorce case. There was a lot of sympathy for that poor devil that got Maybelle first!

"Well," Maybelle said, "if that had been the only time. But then . . . but then . . . there was another, Mister Burns."

"Yes," said the kid.

And he sat down and set his bull-dog jaw and got ready to endure more torture. He got it, too. She didn't leave none of his expectations unfulfilled, I can tell you!

She began to tell that story: "He seemed a poor, haggard, dying man. He had no money. When I met Jeffrey Young, I thought that he would die within a month. And the doctors and his friends thought so, too. Chiefly, they said, because he had nothing that could interest him. There was nothing to hold his mind and his hopes. He was a sad case, Mister Burns, I thought."

I could remember Jeffrey Young. And I don't suppose that he had many interests more than most men, outside of running a string of race horses on the southern tracks, and running a salmon fishery on the mouth of the Columbia for half the year. Outside of those things, and running a set of three houses in three different parts of the country, Jeffrey didn't have very much to fill his mind. He did look like a sick man, but he was just a mite tougher than leather.

Before he got through with running through my mind and my memory, I could hear Maybelle sashaying through to the finish of how that lying Jeffrey Young—she marrying him out of the kindness of her heart—had turned out to be no invalid at all, but just a mean, low . . .

"I can't stand any more," the kid said. "Don't tell me any more. I'm . . . I'm going mad! Missus Wayne . . ."

"Please! Please!" Maybelle cried, covering up her face again. "Not that name."

The kid was knocked fairly woozy.

"And then the third man," Maybelle murmured, "married me, and gave me the name which I loathe and dread . . . and after he married me, he learned to hate me . . ."

"Hate you?" gasped the kid.

"Yes."

"It's not possible," Jigger Bunts said.

"Ah, yes, Mister Burns," Maybelle insisted. "Because some men think that a wife should take part even in the wretched swindling games which their money . . ."

"Lady," the kid interrupted, just white with sickness and disgust and sympathy, "please tell me in one word what it is that you are afraid of? Is it this husband of yours?"

"Yes," Maybelle said, adding, "of him and of his men."

It was a terrible shock to me. I thought that I had warned her that, no matter what she said, she had to keep away from bringing any living men into the danger of the kid. It looked to me as though she had already gone too far in talking about two of her husbands. But now she was getting right down to cases, and I had a pretty uncomfortable feeling for a minute, wondering if she really intended to bamboozle the boy into going out on the warpath?

It didn't seem like Maybelle, but here was the kid turned into a wild man, begging her to tell him where he could find that husband of hers.

"Ah, dear friend," Maybelle said. "I see what you mean. You would rush out and find him, and strike him down like a true knight! But no, I could never again be happy if I felt that any man had been caused to die for my sake. No matter what harms have been done to me." Maybelle paused, looking up to the ceiling. "And no matter how much he pours his scorn and rage and slander around me, I had much rather die myself than have harm come for my sake upon any other living creatures."

It was pretty strong stuff, but the kid swallowed it without getting a raw throat. He was a regular boa constrictor when it came to taking down a lie whole and digesting it quick.

But oh, what a neat gag this was! To whip up the kid with one hand and to rein him with the other. I had to laugh, but I had to admire that girl for being the champion liar of the entire world, which I guess that you'll agree with me when you hear how she worked out the rest of the case against poor old Harry Wayne.

Chapter Twenty-Four

I can't go on telling you how she pulled the wool over the eyes of the poor young idiot, because it makes me blush for being a man to think how any woman could hoodwink one of the same species that I belong to.

I'll just tell you in general what she said to him, which was that Harry Wayne, not being able to use her for his crooked ends, decided thet he would get rid of her.

You would think that the kid would speak up and say: "What was the crooked ends that he intended to use you for? What sort of crookedness was it? Confidence game, or what?"

No sir, he didn't ask any question as sensible as that. The mere idea of asking a question never entered his poor brain. All he done was to rage and groan when she revealed the "wickedness" of poor Wayne.

You see, this was what Wayne had done, according to the girl. He had slid away out to another state, and there he was trying to get a divorce from her. But that wasn't all.

Trying to get that divorce, he had to have bad evidence against her.

"And where on earth could he get that?" cried Jigger Bunts, holding out his hands.

Where could he get it? When I thought of all the ways that a person could get up evidence against poor Maybelle Crofter, it made me fair dizzy, but she was as cool and calm as ever.

"I'll tell you, Mister Burns . . ."

He broke in: "My real name is Bunts. Jigger Bunts, I'm called. I can't hear you calling me by that made-up thing that Tom gave me."

Maybelle done that real well, I have to admitt. She let out a little squeal and got the table and the couch between her and Jigger in a flash. There she stood, apparently scared to death.

"Are you the terrible bandit? Are you the outlaw?" Maybelle asked, seeming to want to squeeze her way through a crack in the wall.

It was a fine thing to see Jigger fold his arms and look grand and calm. He was pretty white, he was so hot.

"They've given me such a reputation, then?" he said. "Even the women are afraid of me?"

She done a quick step around the end of the couch again, and she said: "No, Mister Bunts! No, no I don't care what they say about you. I know how men can lie. And they lie about you, as they've lied about me . . . swearing my reputation away! Swearing yours away. And you're good . . . and kind . . . and true . . . and worthy of being the friend of dear Tom Reynard."

Bah! The smile on his face was like salvation come to a sinner.

"Thank God," Jigger said, very deep and humble. "I thought that this was the end of everything, perhaps. You . . . you seemed to be a thousand miles away from me."

"No," Maybelle said. "This is what draws us close together. We have both been wronged by the world. But oh, Jigger Bunts, how I pity you . . . that a life like yours should be wasted . . . when you are so . . . so good . . . so true . . . so gentle . . . so kind . . ."

"Don't talk about me!" gasped Jigger Bunts. "I don't exist except to help you if God will let me. Only, tell me what that devilish fellow Wayne has dug up against you? And tell me where he has gone to get that divorce. You tell me this!"

She shook her head, very sad and sweet.

"You might go to find him," Maybelle said. "And how could I ever close my eyes in sleep, if I knew that any man had come to harm through me? No, let him go his own way. Except . . . that I do humbly pray that I be shielded from some murderer's hand . . ."

"Murder!" the kid moaned. "Murder! I knew that there would be something like that, before it was done. Do you tell me that what keeps you so frightened in this house . . . so frightened that you dare not kindle even a lamp . . . that you are so hounded with fear because your devilish husband is sending back villains to attempt your life?"

"Ah," Maybelle said. "You are so wonderful!

The very things that I would not have you guess for the whole world, you know at a glance. Oh, Mister Bunts, I have never met a man so brilliant!"

Jigger was not too excited about her to be a little pleased by these remarks about himself. He allowed that if he had been able to see through this deal, it was because he could scent scoundrelism a long distance off.

Then he said: "From now on, you're not to be without some protection. Day and night, I want you to know that there will be someone watching over you. Someone with a strong hand will be near you, God willing, to keep you safe, dear lady!"

Maybelle had dropped back on the couch and looked at him from a great distance, so to speak.

"Oh, Mister Bunts," she said, "I hardly dare to guess what you mean. I hardly dare. I have no right. But do you know what I shall feel tonight?"

"Tell me?" Jigger whispered.

"I shall feel," Maybelle replied, "as though your strong arms were around me, warding me from danger, keeping me safe . . ."

Jigger Bunts pretty near swooned.

Then she told him that she was tired with happiness and that she would have to go to bed, and Jigger went out of that house and foamed away into the darkness like a running horse. He was just as enthusiastic as a small kid with a new game to play.

And that was what I said to myself. But there

was this mighty important difference—the playing of Jigger Bunts was done with a .45 Colt and a real hunting knife and a pair of the hardest fists that ever cracked a jawbone!

I went in to have a chat with Maybelle, and I found her happy but pretty tired.

She sat down on the couch and kicked off her little silver slippers that she had been wearing.

"My feet are spreading as I get older," Maybelle declared.

She stuck out a foot no bigger than a minute.

"I shall have enlarged joints and chilblains," she continued, "if I have to keep up this game with the kid very much longer. Gimme a smoke, Tommy . . . I'm dead for a cigarette."

She made one just a jump faster than a jack rabbit can run, and when it was made, I lighted it for her and watched her lean back in the pillow, drawing in deep breaths and then puffing the smoke out in circles and watching those circles flatten out and curl away against the ceiling. She was smiling while she smoked. And she was looking upward because she didn't want my face to break in on her happy thoughts.

"It was hard work," Maybelle said. "And I'm fagged. Oh, how fagged I am. Tell me how good I was, Tommy, because I'm ready for a little applause."

"Where did you get that lingo?" I asked. "Where did you learn to talk like a book?"

"Some of my husbands educated me," said Maybelle. "They done a good job, too. No trouble to me to put on a high polish that you can see your face in. The kid is full of fancy stuff, too."

"Well," I said, "I'll tell you one thing . . . you're gonna lead a lonely life. You better put up a sign . . . Beware of the Dog. Because when some of your friends come around here, they'll step into trouble up to their necks!"

"What do you mean?" Maybelle asked.

"I mean that you've told the poor fish that you're expecting to be murdered, and when a stray man comes this way, you can lay to it that Jigger will be watching for him!"

"I didn't think of that," Maybelle said.

"You didn't think of a lot of things," I told her. "And among the rest, you didn't think what would happen if he finds out where Wayne has gone to get that divorce."

"Well?" Maybelle considered, frowning at me. "What if he does?"

"There'll be a dead Harry Wayne, that's all . . . if he does find out," I told her.

"A dead Harry Wayne?" Maybelle laughed. "Why, Tommy, Harry Wayne is a man, and a real man. If he met up with this kid, he would turn Jigger Bunts over his knee, give him a spanking, and send him away again with a good lesson."

That explained everything, of course. She hadn't appreciated the facts.

"Maybelle," I said, to sort of break the ground, "will you please tell me how the kid got a reputation like this if he's not a dangerous fighter?"

"Sure, I'll tell you," she answered. "Every gent that wants to, steps out and wears a mask and a Colt to get a reputation. He sticks his miserable little gun in the face of a dozen men, and the dozen men just curl up and throw up their hands and beg him not to kill them. I've met up with some of these desperadoes before, and they're all bunk."

She was so sure that I was sort of paralyzed.

At last I said: "Have you heard what happened this evening?"

She hadn't.

I said: "Do you know Hendon?"

"That brute?" she replied. "Yes, I know him."

"Is he any mama's darling, or is he a fighting fool?"

She gave a little shudder. "I saw him beat up two men with his bare hands, one day. I shall never forget it. He's not a man, but a gorilla."

"All right," I said. "I agree about Hendon. Now lemme tell you what happened. The kid got tired of staying in my room this evening. He eased himself out of the window into a tree that it would break my neck to try to reach. And then he dropped on top of Hendon and five others that were talking underneath the tree about the best way to capture Jigger Bunts. He made a mess of Hendon. He turned the rest of them upside down. And when I came back to the hotel . . . well, you saw him for yourself. Not a mark on him!"

She thought that I was joking, at first, but when I stayed grave, it began to sink in on her.

"Heavens," she said. "Is he as much of a man as all that?"

"That's only an index finger pointing the correct way," I told her. "That's what he can do with his hands. But usually, he doesn't feel at home with his bare hands. He has to have something in his fingers, you know, and when it happens to be a gun, he doesn't miss, Maybelle, not him."

She was more excited than before, now.

"Tommy, Tommy," she cried, "you're telling me that the kid is a *real* man?"

"I'm telling you that," I confirmed. "And I'm telling you that I know Harry Wayne, but if this kid ever goes on his trail, he'll kill poor Harry as sure as God ever made little apples. And killing ain't what you want for Harry, I suppose. Killing ain't the same as alimony, old-timer."

She only stared at me. She was pretty hard hit.

"Heavens above," Maybelle began. "I haven't any malice toward Harry. He's just too decent to have me for a wife. But why didn't you tell me some of these things before?"

"Because I thought that the first time that you met the kid you'd only take a trick or two, and

202

not try to play out the whole game! Maybelle, the thing for you to do is to wrap the kid up in cotton batting and keep him from the air. Because news about Harry Wayne is going to bring about a little man-sized murder!"

Chapter Twenty-Five

When I got back to the hotel there was no Jigger Bunts. There was only a note from him on my table.

Dear Tom,

I wanted to wait here for you and tell you what had happened. But I can't wait. All I can say is that I have found the most wonderful woman in the world and that she has permitted me to try to defend her from some of her troubles. I thank God and you, Tom, for bringing me in her path and I pray that I may be able to undo some of the terrible wrongs which she has suffered from the world. Oh, Tom, what I've learned has made me despise all men, including myself. She is a sacred angel— and she has been treated like a dog. Good bye, Tom, for a little while. I intend to do or to die.

Affectionately,
Jigger

There he was, off in a cloud of glory to his work, and there was I in the hotel, chuckling over my pipe and then hoping a humble hope that maybe the salvation of the kid might be worked out of this deal. If only Maybelle would play the game right—and not lose her head. And if only the kid didn't learn where to find Harry Wayne. That was the main pinch, and I take a little credit to myself for seeing that much in the distance.

I knew that Maybelle would soft pedal on the brutalities of Harry Wayne, for a time, but she had spread an overdose of poison on the subject of Wayne at the first meeting and I knew it would crowd Jigger's system for a long time.

However, I had a good sleep, that night, and then I waked up in the morning to find that there was a new sensation that made poor Jigger Bunts look like a tallow candle by the side of a comet of the first magnitude.

I mean that this was the time of the Garm murders. You recall them—too dog-goned awful and blood-curdling to be repeated here. What paralyzed me and everybody else at the time was the knowledge of Garm. I'd seen Wully Garm myself, not once, but half a dozen times. He was a plain half-wit. Never had done any harm in his life. He was as good a shepherd as a man could ask for, and that was the work that he stuck to.

How he should have got his grudge against the old man that hired him, I don't know. I've always held that Garm's mind just slowly turned from imbecility to insanity. First he had no more mind than a brute. Then the mind that grew up in him became an addled thing, with a devilish leaning toward mischief.

And so the first murder came, and after he had the taste of blood, the others followed as he roved. What made him so frightful hard to catch was just because he could live like a beast, and he could walk through a mountain storm that would've killed an ordinary man. Besides, he had no nerves. When he drew his bead on a target, nothing in the way of mercy ever came between him and the pulling of the trigger. He shot to kill, and he didn't miss because shooting a man was no more to him than shooting a pig.

Bad as New Nineveh was, it was stirred up by the news about Garm. It sent out its contingent to join in the hunt the next day, and I went back to the ranch, from which I had been away longer than I really had any right.

I had a busy ten days, following that, and all that I heard from New Nineveh was two letters from Maybelle.

The first one came at the end of about a week. It ran like this:

Dear Tommy,

The wild man is turning out pretty good. He still acts like I was something on top of an altar, and it is very funny to be treated not like a woman but like a sort of thing made out of china. I might as well be an image, so far as the kid is concerned. He comes to see me every evening after dark. And he tells me that I'm the greatest woman in the world, and bunk like that. It's a scream.

There was pretty near a tragedy the other day, though, and I see that my old Tommy is a pretty good prophet.

It was Ed Smith who dropped in for a talk about old times. I had him in for dinner, and forgot all about the kid. I was having a good party talking to old Ed.

Well, things run along pretty smooth until after dinner Ed got a mite excited and started to kiss me. Well, you know that I never like to be mauled around. Some girls think that it's a great game, but I hate to be fondled like a cat. Poor old Ed thought that I was only joking, I suppose, and then he grabbed me, and I got so mad that I squealed and took a slap at him.

It was all over in a flash.

Something streaked in through the window and a couple of yards of fist and arm shot over my shoulder. The spat of that fist against the face of poor Ed was like two big hands clapped together.

And there lay Ed on the floor and the kid standing over him, trembling.

I was too flabbergasted to do anything, for a minute. I didn't recognize the kid, and his face had something in it that scared me. Just plain murder, Tommy! It was an awful thing to see.

You know that Ed is a big man, but Jigger scooped him up in his arms like a mother carrying a baby. Of course I knew what it meant. He was going to take Ed out into the night and, when Ed waked up, the kid would kill him, because poor old Ed had gone a mite too far with me.

It made me feel pretty sick, but I stopped him.

"Maybelle," says Jigger, "you owe it to the world to let me get rid of this swine of a man. He don't deserve to live."

Well, I was really scared, then, but finally I managed to persuade Jigger that Ed had once been a very good friend of mine and that he really hadn't meant any harm—but that he was just a sort of a simple-minded fellow—you see? I persuaded him at last, but it was a mighty hard fight, I can tell you. And Jigger said that he would let Ed Smith be, if Ed left the house the instant that he got his sense back.

That wasn't happening so quick, either. I swabbed off the blood from Ed's face.

I was all in a tremble, knowing that that young demon was waiting outside in the dark. It really paralyzed me. But it was sort of thrilling, too, to feel that the tiger that chewed up other folks was tame to me, you understand?

When I brought Ed around, I only hoped that he wouldn't talk too much, and he didn't because he's not really the talking kind. I whispered to him that I was sorry, terribly sorry, and I told him that we were watched.

He only gave me a sour grin and then he got himself together and left without a word. Of course he hates my heart, now, and I'll never see him again—which is a shame.

Otherwise, Jigger Bunts has made no trouble. He has fixed himself up in a little room in the top of the barn, a sort of attic, right under the roof. I've been up to see it, today, and it's quite snug. He begged for a picture of mine, and I have given him a couple—which he certainly deserves.

He's just like a child, Tommy. I feel like an old woman when I'm around him and I have to fight like a demon all the time to remember that I'm not that much older than him! That's the way that I dressed the first evening that I saw him, and that's the way that I should never have dressed for him. However, that milk is spilled, and there's no use crying about it.

In the meantime, I have to listen to great yarns about Louis Dalfieri. He worships that man, Tommy. He says that Dalfieri and me are the two great stars that guide his life. You know how he talks, poor kid. Well, I'm terribly fond of him. This lonely life isn't at all bad with him around. Only, I wish that he would treat me as though I were flesh and blood instead of a statue.

I've gotten to such a point that I can drill into him my ideas about the life of an outlaw, and of course I make those ideas pretty strenuous. I tell him that it's a crime for a young man to throw himself away, and I point out the fact that outlawry if nothing else is what makes him skulk like a whipped puppy instead of being able to come to see me in the open day. He seems to see the point of that remark, and I really believe that the noble free life of a two-gun man is not such hot stuff in his eyes as it was when I first saw him.

So long, Tommy.
Maybelle

That was just the sort of a letter that I had wished for. I was glad and surprised to find that there had been only one casualty in the list of Maybelle's men friends. There was only one point that she had failed to cover, and that was whether or not Ed Smith had had a chance to see the face of the man who had knocked him down, and that point was a good deal of importance.

Well, I read that letter once a day. And three days after it came, there was another in the mail from Maybelle. It was shorter and pretty near as exciting as the first one. It said:

Dear Tommy,

Come quick. I have a grand idea that I want to talk over with you. I think that I have a scheme by which the kid can get out of outlawry and back onto his feet again. It's mighty simple. And the best of it is that the same talents that made him a successful bandit may be the means of making him over into an acceptable member of society once more. Hurry and come to me at once. I can't wait to talk it over with you.

Well, I wanted to hurry, but cows are cows, and I had some work waiting for me on the ranch that had to be done first. It was two days before I could make the long trek to New Nineveh, but when I made my start, I didn't hitch a span to a wagon.

I just threw a saddle on the fastest horse on the ranch, that I borrowed from Sam Mitchell's string, and then I made the road smoke all the way from the ranch to New Nineveh, wondering every minute if the delay was going to make it too late for Maybelle to work her fine new plan. And I didn't stop worrying until I pulled up in front of her house and saw the smile on her face when she opened the door to me.

There was still time; that much was plain.

Chapter Twenty-Six

You would have liked to see Maybelle the way that she was that day, full of pep and snap and smiling. She hooked her arm through mine and she led me into her house and sat me down and said to me: "What would you say, Tommy, to making this Jigger Bunts a plumb free man, without the shadow of the law over his poor head?"

I just closed my eyes.

"Maybelle," I said, "ain't I the man that turned him into an outlaw? And of course don't I pray every day that he'll have a chance to get back again where he was when I put him wrong?"

She canted her head on one side, like a dog seeing a new bone. Then she shook her head.

"I'd like to think that," Maybelle said. "I'd like to think that Jigger is such a weakling that he could be molded back and forth by every man that met him. No, Tommy, I think that there was just so much reckless deviltry in Jigger Bunts and that it had to come out sooner or later. Well, you happened to be there to give him a headlong start toward foolishness . . . with that Dalfieri idea."

She gave me a scowl.

"Why, Maybelle," I said, "you got to admit that a man wants to have his joke, now and then."

"Humph!" Maybelle said. "You fellows were grown men, and you took advantage of a mere child."

I didn't answer that with speed at all. I just hauled off and took a good look at Maybelle, to make sure that it was really her that made that remark. Because it didn't sound like her. Beginning with herself and her own affairs, there wasn't much in the world that Maybelle took seriously. But she was serious now.

"However," Maybelle continued, more judge-like than ever, "I know that you're the friend for Jigger. I wish that he had more like you. And I think that I've hit on the way to put him right."

I said: "You mentioned something in your letter about using the same means for setting him right that was used for setting him wrong . . . a fast horse and a pair of Colts. Did you really mean that, Maybelle?"

She didn't seem to hear me. She was sitting there looking past me, with her eyes screwed up, trying to get a distant shot in the future.

"He's able to handle most other men, isn't he?" she asked.

"Like they were children," I told her.

"And after all," Maybelle said, "nothing ventured, nothing won. He's got to take one big chance. But the first thing is a trip for you to see the governor."

"Me? The governor?" I gasped. "That would be

a treat to him, to have a chance to sit down and talk to me, wouldn't it?"

"You ain't funny, Tommy," Maybelle insisted, very cold. "You're just silly, you understand? You're too modest to go and see the governor. But you weren't too honest to start in and run the poor kid hell-ward as fast as you and your gang of second-rate jokers, as you call yourselves, could do it."

Well, I couldn't believe that I was hearing her straight, because not a word of that lingo sounded a bit like the Maybelle Crofter that I knew, and that was such a good pal and square-shooter.

She left me flabbergasted, and then she went on: "You're to go to the governor, however, as fast as you can get, and when you arrive there, you're going to break in and see him, if you have to kill a couple of flunkies to get at him. And when you see him, you're going to get five minutes of his listening time even if you have to take it at the point of your Colt. And you're going to say to him . . . 'Boss, do you want to be a mighty popular governor down in my neck of the woods?' And when he says yes, you're going to say to him . . ."

Well, I won't tell you here what it was that Maybelle suggested to me. It was a rank thing to try on the governor of a state and at first I said that it wouldn't work, at all, but she insisted until

I gave in, and, after that, the more that I thought about the deal, the more I felt that it might work.

I had a thirty mile cross-country ride to get me to the right railroad to run to the capital of the state. But I made the ride on a fresh horse that I borrowed from Maybelle, and then I sat up all night, bumping over a mountain roadbed in a day coach that was filled with reprobates that had got themselves all filled up with *vino*. Funny thing how long it lasted those fellows. Of course, they got themselves as chock-a-block as a pot of blotters dipped in water. And every time anything happened, it just squeezed some more noise and good nature out of them. Those idiots, they didn't mind the jolting of that car. And when the brakes went on with a wham! and piled up half a dozen of them on one end of the coach, they just picked themselves up, laughing, and they started singing a song. They knew all the songs that there were in the world outside of the English language, and they sung them so good that you wouldn't believe it. They kept it up to the crack of dawn, and then just as they began to sober up enough to fall asleep in patches, here and there, the train pulled into the capital town.

But, oh my, I wouldn't've had the heads that those muckers would own by the time that they got to the end of that day's trip and the mines where they were to start working, right away!

I got out and I had my eye full of the city right away. I have been to Denver, but that's just too big to understand. It's like a world all by itself. It would take you a year just to memorize the names of the streets, and even then you wouldn't know half of them! You could bust around and eat in a different place—a hotel or a restaurant—every day pretty near forever.

But Denver, as I say, is too big to understand. But the state capital, it had only about twenty-five thousand, which you'll agree is a whopping big town. It had street cars, and pavements, and electric lights, and shops with wax models in the windows, and businessmen that wore rubber-heeled shoes and bright polishes, and high-stepping horses, and pretty near everything that you could ever wish to see. But I'll tell you, you could only hope to learn to understand a town like that, if you was to live the biggest part of your life in it!

I was terrible interested, and when I went up to the big white stone building where the governor's office was, I hardly minded it when they told me that I would have to have an appointment made with his secretary before I could talk to him. I went in to see his secretary, which was a young man that smiled a good deal, but it didn't seem to mean much, and he hoped that he would see me again, but he didn't give me much hope that I would see the governor, which he said was suffering a lot from having shaken so many hands the week before at a reception. He kept right on talking until he talked me out of his office and I went back and wandered around the town again.

Altogether, I was pretty well satisfied that there was only one way to manage, and that was to break in on the old governor when he wasn't expecting me.

I walked out to his house that afternoon. And I walked around it until I had a pretty good idea of the lay of the land. I saw a man polishing the brass on the front door on which there was a hook-nosed knocker and much trumpery all around, you understand? I told him that it was a mighty big house and that it must be a fine thing to work in such a big place. He said that it was, but that if I was looking for a job, it was no good, because there was a waiting list. I said I was sorry to hear that because I had heard it was fine to work for such a kind-hearted man as the governor.

He said: "Where did you hear that? The chief is made out of horse-hide and iron. That's all. He's so mean that he don't even mind the sunshine in the morning and he sleeps on the east side of the house with the blinds all up!"

That was a good deal to learn, and that night I waited around in the back garden of the house for the light to flash on in that big set of windows on the second floor. However, I didn't have to do no porch climbing, after all.

Just before midnight, the governor and his wife came out for a breath of fresh air, as they put it, and they walked up and down with the moon on their silvery hair. What would you think that important folks like that would talk about? Important things, of course. Well, you would've been surprised!

"What a damned old bore the judge is!" the governor said to his wife.

"Would you mind not walking so fast?" said the governor-ess.

"Are your feet sore from those infernal tight shoes?" the governor asked.

"My shoes are not tight!" she said. "Heavens . . . at my age I hope that vanity . . ."

"Stuff!" he exclaimed. "There are a lot of queer things about you, Lizzie, but nothing quite so queer as your ideas about yourself. The trouble with women is that . . ."

"Harry," she said, "I've sat on platforms and listened to your silly speeches, but I won't listen to them in my own backyard. I'm going inside for a little peace!"

"Humph!" was the governor's response to that. And he let her go in.

Well, there you are! There was a couple of newspapers that always printed pictures of the governor and his wife with their two grandchildren on their laps, and their growed up sons and daughters standing grouped around, trying to look like they didn't know that they were in the papers. Thousands of votes the size of that family got for the governor. Because you take a big family man like that, people take it for granted that he hasn't got such a lot of fancy brains, you know. It looks solid and simple. You even feel a little superior to him, and a little pity for him. And that's the sort of people that we Americans like to elect to office to run us.

The governor threw away his cigarette as soon as his wife was gone inside of the house and he got out an old black pipe and whittled up some plug and stuffed that pipe and lighted it up, and I tell you what, that pipe was a snorter, even out there in the open airs I got a lot more respect for the governor right away. Then he walked up and down with a frown on his forehead, and the moon on his face, and his hands folded behind him.

"Now he is working out a pretty important point," I mutter to myself, but just then he began to move his lips and then I heard him singing very soft.

Hey, diddle diddle,
The cat and the fiddle,
The cow jumped over the moon.
The little dog laughed to see such sport
And the dish . . .

I got a whiff of his pipe smoke, and it brought a sneeze ripping out of me before I could do anything to control it. The governor turned around with a grunt, and there was me stepping out of the shrubbery behind him.

He made a grab at his hip pocket, and gave a little squeal of excitement, more like a pig than a governor, but I made free to grab his right wrist.

"Chief," I warned, "let's talk it over friendly. I don't mean you no harm at all."

He was as cool as the devil, after the first fluster.

"I don't think you do," he says. "But why are you back here like a sneak thief?"

"Because your secretary says that you're engaged until the end of the year."

"God bless him," the governor said more to himself than me. "The tonnage of lying that he's able to do would sink an ocean liner. Well, sir, what do you want of me now that you have me? I only make one bargain with you . . . that you don't keep me here more than ten minutes."

Chapter Twenty-Seven

That was a pretty fair bargain. Ten minutes was really enough for me to tell my yarn in, and as I accepted, the governor pulled out his watch and wound it, looking me in the face.

"Now," he said, "what do you want?"

"I'm here," I explained, "to make a bargain for an outlawed man."

The governor was pleased right away. He dropped the watch into his vest pocket and put his hands on his hips. He looked a square-shooter.

"Who's your man?" he asked.

"Jigger Bunts," I told him.

The governor shook his head. "You're aiming to die," said he. "I don't mind being held up for the sake of some common or garden criminal. I have a lot of sympathy with the crooks. Every honest man ought to have, if he's taken enough fair looks into his *own* heart. But in the meantime, what I want to know is how I could strike any sort of a bargain with a desperado who has been making fools out of my sheriffs, laughing at our posses, and cramming the newspapers with accounts that make the law and the governor of the state look very foolish indeed. No, sir, you can't talk to me about a fellow like Bunts, who I have an almost personal grudge against. I don't mind saying that

I feel a record like his is a blot on the record that I have made as an officer upholding the law with my whole strength!"

That was pretty much of a facer for me, but I wasn't to be beaten off at the very beginning.

I said: "Your honor, you were under twenty, once."

"Don't talk to me like a judge," he said, and grinned. "Yes, I was once under twenty. What follows from that?"

"Nothing, except that you know that when a man is under twenty, he's apt to be a good deal of a fool."

The governor grinned.

"Do you know that Jigger Bunts was under twenty when he started?" I asked.

"Billy the Kid was only thirteen or fifteen when he started," said the governor. "But he killed more than one white man for every year of his life, before he was through with his career. And there were Negroes and Indians and Mexicans thrown in for full measure without being counted at all. No, sir, I know that some of these rascally gunfighters are precocious, but that doesn't incline me to be more merciful. What is your name?"

"Tom Reynard."

"Reynard," the governor repeated. "I've never heard your name before, but you've got a clean pair of eyes in your head and you ought to know that a gunfighter is a detestable cur, as a rule. He spends his life practicing with his weapons, instead of working honestly. And when he can think of nothing else to do, he starts out and finds himself a fight. What chance would I have against a real gunfighter? I can't hit the side of a barn with a revolver, and I'm inclined to thank God for it. Rifles are meant to bring down game. But revolvers bag nothing but human beings . . . and I wish that the sale of them were prohibited by a most stringent law!"

It was my luck to run into a governor for our state who was so red hot against desperados and gunfighters.

"Well, sir," I said, "I want to ask you to remember in the first place that you can't count the time that you talk out of my ten minutes."

He wasn't offended. He chuckled and nodded. "I guess I've been at the stump again," he admitted. "It's a bad habit that we politicians have. We can't think except in headlines. Go on, Mister Reynard."

He was a real good one, was that governor. The sort that you wouldn't mind having in camp, even in winter. You could lay to it that he would lift his share of the work.

I said: "You got to make a distinction between a gunfighter and a man who shoots straight."

"Perhaps, perhaps," he said. "But what are you driving at?"

"Well, I want you to notice that the kid . . .
I mean, Jigger Bunts . . . shoots so dog-goned
straight that he hasn't killed a man yet . . ."

"Hold on! He's wanted for murder!" barked the
governor.

"That was a sneaking head-hunter . . . a no-good
swine!" I let him know. "No district attorney in
the state would dare to try him for that. The jury
would wind up by voting the kid their thanks, I
tell you. No, I want to get a pardon for the other
fracases, but I'd as soon see him step to the tune
for that killing!"

The governor was pretty interested, by this
time.

"Are you an uncle of Bunts?" he asked.

Then I opened up and I told the story. As fast
as I could, but even at that, the story didn't fit
into any short space of time. I tell you, I left out
nothing, from the first time I met the kid, up to
the time that I said good bye to Maybelle. The
governor listened like a good sort. He laughed at
me and Louis Dalfieri until there was tears in his
eyes.

Then he said: "Reynard, this is the queerest
story that I've ever heard in my life. I'm flabbergasted. But I believe every word that you've said.
But what can I do? I'd like to help that boy. I'd . . .
I'd like to have a talk with him, even. But show
me a loophole through which I can step with any
dignity and pardon him."

"I'm going to make you a loophole," I said. "This Jigger Bunts isn't the only critter that's roaming around in this here state and messing up the face of the law and cramming the newspapers."

"It's true," the governor agreed.

"Now," I told him, "suppose that I get Missus Wayne to take this job up with the kid and to tell him that he has to make his peace with the law and to start him after one of these crooks . . . these real crooks, that shoot to kill every time they get their fur up? If he brings in one of those badmen, dead or alive, will you write him a pardon?"

He considered this thing up and down. "It's damned illegal!" he hissed.

"But natural," I said.

"Tell me, is this Missus Wayne's idea?"

"Yes," I said. "Every word of it. I wouldn't have the nerve to think out a whole idea like that."

"Humph," the governor said, adding: "You go back and tell her to go ahead. If your man Bunts can land Croydon, the counterfeiter, or that scoundrelly kidnapper, Loftus, or, of course, the abysmal brute, Wully Garm, I'll sign a pardon for him. Will that suit you?"

I said that it would—that it would suit me all over, and I couldn't help throwing in that it would make me and a lot of other honest men the friends of that governor for life.

"Humph," he repeated. "Now about this Missus Wayne. What's to become of her?"

"She'll have her divorce and be free, in a little while," I told him. "Then she can go on making business for the lawyers, I suppose."

"Perhaps," he said. "But I wonder if mothering this Jigger Bunts may not make everything else pretty dull for her?"

I had never thought of that, and I told the governor that the whole thing was just a joke.

"A joke?" he exclaimed. "Now let me tell you, Reynard, that you're old enough to know that women have no sense of humor . . . inside their own affairs. They're too damned serious, even the best of them, and you put that idea in your pipe and smoke it for a while, will you? But as for this business, you've taken an hour of my time, not ten minutes. Good night, Reynard. God be with you and the boy. I wish you all the luck in the world!"

He was such a straight shooter, so simple and so damned fine, that it just brought the tears to my eyes. I shook hands with him, and then I went to find a hotel.

The next morning, I was driving south as fast as a train would carry me, and that same night I was in the house of Maybelle again. What would you think that I walked in on?

Well, it was Jigger Bunts sitting in a corner of

227

the room with his mustaches more waxed out than ever and Maybelle had a book under her arm when she opened the door to me and led me in.

"Hello," I said, after I'd shaken hands with Jigger. "Are the pair of you back in school? What's the book?"

"The most wonderful book in the world," Maybelle gushed. "It's all about Tristram and Lancelot and Arthur and Guinevere, and the rest of them. They were a happy lot of high-steppers, Tommy! Sit down while I read to you and Jigger about . . ."

"Have you been reading aloud?" I asked.

"Yes," she said, "and never had such a . . ."

I just stood there and wondered at her, because I knew that the only reading that she every cottoned onto was the ads in the fashion magazines, and such like things. But here she was sober enough to do knitting, and wearing glasses!

I cut in on that reading and pulled her to one side.

"It's fixed," I told her. "Garm . . . or Loftus . . . or Croydon, the counterfeiter, dead or alive. Garm doesn't count, of course. Don't sic the kid after him, because Garm is too damned dangerous, even for the kid. But if he fetches in either of the other two . . . dead or alive . . . there's a pardon waiting for him in the governor's office. You understand?"

"Thank God," said Maybelle. "Then he's saved."

"There's only one dead gunfighter between him and another even start," I said.

And I left her to work up the idea with the kid in her own way, because there was something about this bartering of one life for another that I didn't like, particular, as you may understand for yourself.

It had been a rough, long trip, and an anxious one, and I was mighty glad to hit the hay that night.

The next day I sashayed out to the ranch without even stopping to call on Maybelle before I left. I didn't have to. There had been something close and chummy in the air of the room the night before that made me know that what one of them wanted, the other would be sure to try to do.

But all the way out to the ranch, I kept remembering what the governor had said—that the kid wasn't the only one to be thought of in this game. And that Maybelle counted, too, and counted pretty big! Perhaps he was right. How right he was, I never guessed till the end.

Chapter Twenty-Eight

What happened was what we might have known beforehand, if we had used any sense. When we turned loose the kid, like a hawk he sighted the biggest quarry and went after it.

He had Loftus and Croydon, big enough quarry for any man, you would say, but the kid had a different opinion. I got part of the history from Jigger himself and part from others. And part of it you could deduce from what was known.

Before Maybelle got through with him that night, there didn't seem anything strange in bringing in one man to stand for him—turning over one outlaw to take the place of the kid's own danger. He was off in the dark, before morning, riding hard, but the direction that he picked was not that in which Croydon or Loftus had been seen last. He galloped for the region where the brute—Wully Garm—was last seen.

Even Jigger Bunts must have felt some fear while he was riding on that trail. He wouldn't've been human if he hadn't. But he got into the mountains just after the worst of all of Garm's crimes had been committed—I mean the murder of the three Chippendales in their ranch house. No reason for that killing. Wully was simply running amuck, now, and killing for the sake of the slaughter!

Jigger Bunts followed the trail of Garm, hard and fast, and he came about even of the fourth day from the Chippendale house, in sight of the carcass of a deer. The way that deer had been butchered was so rough and showed such a strong hand that the kid made up his mind, on the spot, that Wully Garm must have done that work. And having done that work, it occurred to Jigger that Wully would probably have eaten a belly full and gone into the woods somewhere pretty near to sleep off his meal.

Well, Jigger was a great hand at following a trail. Under some fallen leaves he picked up the mark of a great sprawling foot and in ten minutes of careful work, he came onto the sound of a heavily breathing creature. When he stepped out into a little clearing and in the shadow at one side of it, he had his first view of Garm.

It must have been a horrible thing to see that great loose-lipped face even when it was quiet in sleep. And Jigger told me afterward that the face was *not* really quiet, but working a little all of the time—the jowls quivering, or the big lips twitching a bit, or the fleshy brow being disturbed into a wrinkle.

Just the way that a wild dog acts by the fire— jerking open an eye every now and then and looking around out of his sleep with a start.

But, anyway, there was Wully Garm found at last, the whole two and a half shapeless hundred-weight of him. I think that if I'd been the lucky fellow who made that discovery, I should have put a bullet through his head while he lay there and never let him see the light of the stars again.

And even the bravest man wouldn't have wanted to do anything bolder than to tie the hands of the giant while he was sleeping. But that wouldn't suit Jigger.

Louis Dalfieri, according to the yarns that the boys and me told about him, would always fight any man in any way that he wanted to fight, and with any weapons. And so the kid sat down on a rock and waited while the moon rose and shone bright over the trees.

At last, there was a grunt and a snort, and the sleeper was awake, and rolling to his knees.

He wasn't confused. He was too near to the brute to have his brain numbed by sleeping, but, like a wolf, the moment he opened his eyes, he was himself.

He reached for his revolver—his rifle—his knife.

They were all gone, of course. The kid had had the sense to see to that.

Jigger stood facing the big, squat beast of a man, and he said: "Garm, I've come to take you to jail. Will you go along quietly?"

Garm showed his yellow, pointed teeth.

Imagine asking Garm to come along to jail! However, that was the way of the heroes in the books that the kid had always been reading. And that would have been Louis Dalfieri's way, of course. He was going to be knightly or bust.

"Do you hear me?" Jigger said, with a shudder going through him, I suppose, as he saw the brute stand up on its hind legs and snarl at him.

"I hear you," Garm said. "But I'm not going. If I got to be murdered, I'll be murdered here."

"Murdered?" the kid said, and I can see how his head would have gone up and how his lip would have curled. "Murdered? There's to be no murder, Wully Garm. We'll fight it out fair and square in any way that you choose."

Of course, Garm wouldn't believe him. But when he finally got the idea through his head, he went almost crazy with joy, and reached out his long arms and his great thick, wiggling fingers.

"No guns . . . no knives . . . hands!" Garm shouted, and his mouth gaped with a wolf's grin. "Hands, hands!"

And what did Jigger do?

Oh, he simply threw aside guns and knives and rifle and all, and he stood up to the giant with his bare hands!

"I'm glad that I didn't see that fight. It must have been too horrible. Not like man and man, but like an eagle and a bear, say. With Garm the bear and the kid the eagle.

The kid tried to close with his man and grapple. I suppose he felt that the only real knightly thing was to do just exactly as Garm did, but the instant that those great fingers closed on him, he knew his mistake.

I knew that the kid could turn himself into a greased snake, when he wanted to get away from anyone. I'd seen him do it at the ranch, when half a dozen of the boys tried to get him down, but he would have died this time, if, as he twisted about, his shirt hadn't torn to threads and so let him out of the hands of Garm, half naked. Garm rushed on in, fair slavering with joy and running on his great, crooked, thick legs.

He caught at the thin air and got a blind pair of slashing punches across the face. The kid stood off and began to box. He slammed Garm with both hands until his arms ached, but he couldn't put the big fellow down.

He cut the face of Garm simply to ribbons, and the pain addled whatever little wits there were left to big Wully Garm.

I suppose that he would have been sure to win out in this sort of fighting, if he had just waited long and patiently enough. Because the cutting hands of the kid might hurt and sting him, but they couldn't do him any real harm, any more than the talons of an eagle could do any harm to a bear.

But Wully couldn't stand the gaff. Finally, he

reached down and caught up a rock the size of half a man's body and heaved it at the kid. The corner of it brushed his head and knocked him flat, and Garm rushed in to finish his job.

He rushed in, but here the luck was against him just as he was aiming to finish the fight in grand style by falling on the kid and choking the life out of him with one mangling grip of his big hands.

He had made a mistake, as I was saying, because the spot where the kid dropped, half stunned, was where he had shed his guns when he shed them in standing up to face the challenge of Garm. And when the active hand of the kid fell on the cold steel of his Colt, there was a flash of light let into his brain.

Or maybe that hand of his acted almost automatically, it had been so well trained by Jigger Bunts for hour after hour, and for day after day.

And so, as Wully Garm threw himself through the air at the kid, the hand of Jigger Bunts flicked out faster than the tongue of a snake and it came back carrying a .45 Colt that barked right into the hideous face of Garm.

Afterward, Jigger lay for a time, sick and done for. But he managed to pull himself out from under the weight of the dead. He was exhausted. But except for the scratch along his head, he wasn't badly hurt.

When he was rested, he went back to his horse, and he rode on down to the nearest town.

"Is there an officer of the law in this place?" the kid asked the first person he saw.

The gent that had met up with him said there was, because a deputy sheriff had just come up there from New Nineveh on the trail of Wully Garm, and right now he was at the hotel.

To the hotel went Jigger and walked straight in.

It made a pretty good picture I'll bet, and I'll never forgive my luck for not giving me a chance to see it.

There stands Jigger Bunts, with the dust and the dirt brushed off of him, and his coat buttoned up high, and the big flowing black necktie done around his throat because his shirt had been torn to pieces. But he had gone over the rest of himself, and rubbed out and twisted his mustaches to as sharp a point as ever, and had combed his hair, and tied a handkerchief around the place on his head where the corner of the big stone had cut through to the skull.

And yonder stood Hendon, whose face was still swollen and purple and out of shape from the beating the kid had given him not so terribly long before.

Hendon let out a bellow and grabbed out two Colts. Gents who were there at the time say that his hands shook a lot, and he was so excited he probably couldn't have hit the wall, let alone Jigger Bunts.

However, Jigger hadn't come there to find more

trouble. He just smiled at Hendon and said: "I've come to surrender myself, Hendon, and to tell you that your chase of Garm is ended."

"Ended?" Hendon repeated, fair paralyzed, of course. "Has the brute fallen off a cliff?"

"More or less," the kid answered. "I'll tell you where to find him laid out."

Chapter Twenty-Nine

Hendon came tearing back to New Nineveh like a conquering hero, with Jigger Bunts along with him, and he timed his entry so as to make it about noon, when everybody could come out into the streets and see him go by with his rifle balanced across the pommel of his saddle and Jigger all covered with irons and guarded by gents with naked guns, riding behind.

Hendon got a lot of cheers for that bit of work. People sort of overlooked the fact that Jigger had come in and given himself up. And when that was suggested, Hendon allowed that Jigger had been *scared* into surrendering, because he knew that he, Hendon, was on the trail.

Anyway, there wasn't a long time left for Hendon to lick his chops. The papers were all full of the news the next morning, and the message was telegraphed through to New Nineveh that evening.

It was all full of whereas's—extreme legal. And it set out that, since Jigger had only one death laid to him, and that being the death of another man in bad order with the law, and since he had voluntarily submitted to arrest and showed a willingness to stand trial and submit to punishment for his crimes, and most of all because he had done a lot for the people of the mountains by killing the murderer, Wully Garm, the governor felt that young Bunts was the sort of stuff out of which a good citizen could be made with a little care, and, above all, because Jigger had found out that he was not as strong as the law.

Well, that wasn't a popular message in the town of New Nineveh. Maybe there was a lot to be said on the side of Jigger Bunts, but New Nineveh wanted the pleasure of having the trial and the hanging of a famous man to its credit and right in its midst. But certainly there was one man that didn't flourish on the news that the kid was to be turned loose.

That was Hendon. He developed business in the far corner of the county, right away, and he rode off the morning that the kid was released. Everyone knew it was because Hendon had been talking a little bit too free, and he didn't want to meet up with Jigger and have the kid ask him some pointblank questions.

Anyway, there was only one important thing to me. I came hiking into town as fast as I could whack the miles out of a tough-mouthed mustang and I headed straight for the house of Maybelle Wayne, because I figured for sure that the kid would go there as soon as he got loose from the jail.

I found Maybelle, but Jigger hadn't come,

as yet. Maybelle was so excited that she was shaking. She was half laughing and half crying, and I shook hands with her hard enough to break bones.

"Maybelle," I said, "I don't give a damn what some folks hold against you. You've done such a good job of the kid that it would outbalance all the rest. I want to say that . . ."

She wasn't even interested in praise. She just broke in, hollering: "But he ought to be here! Why doesn't he come, Tommy? Why doesn't he come?"

She was actually walking up and down and wringing her hands. And her the coolest headed woman that ever stepped!

I remembered then for the hundredth time what the governor had said.

"Maybelle," I said to her, "do you mean to tell me that you've gone off your balance about this youngster . . . this kid, Jigger?"

"Bah!" she said in reply. "You make me tired, Tom Reynard! Who brought that kid to me? I'm flesh and blood, ain't I? And wouldn't anything human go crazy about him?"

It knocked me dizzy!

"All right," I said. "But you'll get over it quick enough. You'll get over it, easy. You've got over things like this before."

She laughed in my face.

"You don't know nothing, dearie," Maybelle

said. "The rest were all pikers or meal tickets, or something, but this kid is the real thing. Get over it? I'll be dead and buried before I'm over it, Tommy."

"My God," I muttered, "you're really in love at last."

Because I never would've believed it of her. She was a good pal and fine company, and all of that. But when it came to love . . . why, it didn't seem to be in her. It was something that she knew about and looked at from a distance, and could always laugh at.

But now here she was leaning up against the wall with her hands over her heart and her head back and her eyes closed.

And she said through her stiff lips: "Love him? Yes, I love him. And always have from the first moment that I saw him."

"You laughed when you first saw him," I reminded her.

"I laughed for happiness, because I knew that he was real, and that I would get such a hold on him that he'd never get away. You understand, Tommy? Never get away! I'd . . . I'd kill him rather than let another woman have him. I don't want him to know other women. I don't want him to know men. I want to fill up his life. And I'll make him happy. Oh, God, Tommy, I'll pour out my heart like water for him. I'd want to die for him. I love him, and love him, and love him. It's fire in me . . . it'll kill me unless he comes soon! Go find him, Tommy. Quick, quick . . . because he'd be here with me before this if something serious hadn't happened. Go Tommy . . . go quick!"

She just pushed me out of the house and I went down toward the hotel feeling pretty groggy.

I still couldn't believe it. I still couldn't believe that Maybelle had lost her head about any man, least of all about a youngster like Jigger . . . not just five years younger than she was, but fifty years younger. If he lived to be half a century older, he would never be as old as she was, because he didn't have the kind of a mind that got old. He would stay young, half foolish, likeable, and silly and grand and proud and star-gazing all his life, but Maybelle was born wise and had got wiser and wiser. There was nothing that she couldn't see through—except this one thing— love. Or blindness, you might call it. Because that's what love seems to be.

When I got downtown, I asked for Jigger Bunts, and the boys just laughed at me.

"He's gone hunting for Hendon," they said. "He just pulled out of town bound west on the train. And Hendon rode off in the same direction."

That was a wild bit of news to me.

I couldn't understand it. I knew that Jigger got ideas quick, and that he acted on them quicker.

But it never entered my head that he would leave New Nineveh before he had seen me and Maybelle, and all for the sake of getting even with a no-account fellow like Hendon. No, I wiped Hendon off the books. There just had to be some other reason.

I got one, too, mighty quick. When I asked how he happened to start so soon, Bosco Jones, that run the hotel, told me that the kid had heard somebody mention Harry Wayne's ranch and Jigger had turned around and said: "Where's Harry Wayne now?"

"In Nevada," said the cowpuncher, "in Carson City."

"Are you sure?" Jigger asked.

"Ain't I just mailed a letter to him?" said the puncher. "As sure as I'm working for him."

And the first thing that you know, he had ripped out the name of the hotel where Harry Wayne was staying.

Well, when I heard that, I knew. The westbound train might go in the same direction that Hendon had ridden out of town that morning. But it also went on a long distance past the place where Hendon was riding for. It went on to Carson City. And I knew the reason. The worst pile of danger that ever came toward Harry Wayne was headed for him now, and, unless he got help, he would be finished before another twenty-four hours.

You could see how the kid figured everything.

He owed his return to a free life out of fear of the law to the wise ideas of Maybelle, and before he even so much as went to her to thank her for what her brains had done for him, he was going to manage to pay her back, if he could.

And how could he pay her back? Why, by making her as free as he was, and by removing the gent that was slandering her, and divorcing her, and hiring rascals to go after her peace and her good name! By killing Harry Wayne, he would be doing a good deed for the world and he would be repaying the girl that he loved— worshipped, would be the better word. Because I know now that Maybelle as a woman never even entered the mind of the kid. She stepped in as a goddess, and nothing else.

Well, I did three things quick.

I wrote down the street address of Wayne in Carson City, just as I had got it from the hotelkeeper.

Then I hiked to the telegraph office and wired to Wayne:

WATCH YOURSELF. KEEP UNDER COVER. YOU ARE RUNNING INTO DANGER FOR YOUR LIFE.

Then for the third thing, I started to find Maybelle.

She didn't need a pair of opera glasses to read

the importance of that news that I was bringing her. She knew right away that it was likely to be the beginning of the end—though of what sort of an end, she couldn't guess, of course.

"If he kills Wayne, Jigger is no better than a dead man himself," she cried, scared white, I can tell you. "Because Harry Wayne is no common man and his killing would make a terrible stir. Tommy, you and me have to start for Carson City, and we start right now. Oh, I wish that I'd never been born! But how could I ever have guessed . . ."

It wasn't like her to talk like that. But I didn't stop to ask questions or to wonder at things like that. I hot-footed it to the station and there I got some good news—that if we waited an hour more, we'd get an express that would hike overland and arrive at Carson City that night about eleven o'clock—a whole hour ahead of the jerkwater local that the kid was traveling on.

I busted back to Maybelle with the news, and you can bet that when the overland pulled out of New Nineveh that afternoon she may have had a lot more important people aboard her, but she didn't have no more anxious ones.

Chapter Thirty

We were right on time, and the way that we rolled along and clicked off the miles with the truck and the spinning wheels chuckling along under the train was a caution. And the yellow dust clouds flurried up past the windows on one side, and the white smoke scooped down on the other side. You couldn't open a window on either side without getting your eyes and nose and neck and lungs all full of fine Nevada sand and that smoke.

All that we could do was sit there and stifle and sweat and begin to stick to the seat and turn red and get mean, and start hating the whole world, and each other most of all. That was the way that the trip started, but, really, we didn't care much about the heat down in our hearts. All that we minded was the swift, smooth, steady way in which the miles were rattling out behind us.

All that afternoon we did fine, and during that time we climbed most of the grades, but in the evening—it was twilight at the time—we had to stop.

"There's no station!" Maybelle saw, shaking all over. "Go out and see what's happened, Tommy."

I went out and dragged in a couple of breaths of the luke warm air of that Nevada evening. I found out what was wrong. A hot box.

"It'll be all right," I told Maybelle when I went back inside. "They'll get this thing fixed up, and, as soon as they do, we'll snake along so fast that it'll make your head swim, I tell you."

That was what I had hoped, but my hopes didn't pan out. For three hours we crawled. And I'm not going to write about those three hours. Maybelle had more nerve and more courage than any man or woman that I've ever known, but that nerve petered out, here. She couldn't stand the gaff, and I watched her lying with her head back against the seat, looking half sick and half ready to be hysterical, and very pale of cheek and red of nose.

She wasn't pretty. She was homely. She was homely as the devil, that afternoon. But the wonderful thing was that I knew one glimpse of the kid would make her even prettier than ever.

I got to wondering, too. Even if the kid did marry her—after her divorce—he might do worse. Because I didn't have any doubt now. She was going to be straight with him, and she would never stop loving him till she was in her grave. She had said that and I knew that it was true.

Well, at last they made a change, and we started to make up time. But there wasn't much use. We got in ten minutes past midnight. Maybe the local had been delayed, too.

I jumped for the porter and shook half his wits

out of his head, but he stammered out that the local had come in right on the stroke of midnight. And that was that.

We got a cab and went zooming for the hotel, with me sticking my head out of the window and cussing that driver and telling him that his horses were going to sleep between steps.

We got to the hotel and at the desk the night clerk told me that Mr. Wayne had left the hotel two days before, because he expected to be in Carson City some time and had rented a little cottage on the outskirts of the town.

"Has a young chap been here . . . about ten minutes ago?" I asked the clerk.

"Yes," he said, "and he went on . . ."

"Gimme the address of the Wayne house . . . life or death!" I shouted.

I got it and I made one jump to the door of the hotel and one more into the cab.

Then we started out again, just as fast as those horses could wing it along the streets. We sounded like a cavalry charge. And the echoes, they came flying and ringing and spattering around our ears.

We got to the house. I was out before the cab was stopped, and Maybelle was right there beside me, running.

There was a dark streak of young poplar trees, and behind them there was a little pink and blue stucco house—more like a girl would pick out

248

than what a big rough-neck rancher like Harry Wayne would be expected to want.

"It's quiet . . . there's no noise . . . thank God," observed Maybelle.

I heard the last of that dying out behind me as I started sprinting. I cleared the hedge right in my stride like a hurdler, I made one jump to the middle of the lawn, and then I pulled up short, because right in front of me the big window was open and there at opposite sides of the table was Harry Wayne and Jigger Bunts. Perhaps Jigger had not been ten minutes in the house, but he had done enough in that time to make himself known. Harry Wayne was dabbing a handkerchief at a bloody place on his face but he paid little attention to that, and, one by one, he was shoving certain papers across the table to Jigger.

They were the proofs of the guilt of Maybelle—the same proofs with which Harry was winning his divorce suit, of course—and that they were damning, I could see in the face of the kid. I heard a caught breath at my side—there was Maybelle, seeing all that I saw, and understanding, too.

And now we saw Jigger Bunts drop his head into his hands and cover his face. He had seen too much!

I felt a twitch at my coat and turned in time to see Maybelle with my Colt in her hand. I thought that what she intended was to take a pot shot at Harry Wayne, and I jumped in her way. Because

I knew that there was temper and spirit enough in that girl to lead her to try almost anything. But I was wrong. It wasn't Wayne that she intended to use the gun on.

Before I could stir a hand, she clapped that gun against her head and fired!

It was sort of fitting, in a way, that it was Jigger Bunts who got to her first and picked her up in his arms. He carried her into the house and put her on the bed of Harry Wayne. She was still breathing, and her heart was fluttering, though how she could live after such a wound I couldn't guess. It seemed to me that the slug must have passed straight through her brain, but as we washed the wound and examined it more carefully, we could see how the bullet had turned against the skull and glanced away.

And who was the man there that felt the most sorrow for Maybelle?

Well, I'm ashamed to say that it wasn't me. Because as I looked things over, it seemed to me that Maybelle had saved Jigger Bunts from himself, and with that bullet she had tried to turn Harry Wayne free, also. And if she had to die, there was no better time than this, before she did anything else more foolish.

It wasn't Jigger who grieved the most. In that second when he covered up his face with his hands, he must have been wracked with grief and disgust by what Harry Wayne had told him, and proved to him. At any rate, as he leaned over Maybelle, he looked five years older, and a century sterner, but there was no tenderness in him.

He helped to take care of her wound, and he did a better job than either of the others of us who were there, but that was simply because he did *everything* better than we could manage it. But all the time he was as cold as ice. He was like a doctor with a charity case on his hands, and a damned disagreeable one, at that.

Well, as I watched Jigger at that moment, I saw what was wrong with him. He couldn't stand reality. He had to have a dream made to order for him by someone else, and then he would live in the middle of that dream perfectly happy. But show him the facts in the daylight, and he was done for—he wasn't interested.

Who was the hardest hit? It was Harry Wayne who was the hardest hit.

The blood was still trickling down his face from the place where Jigger Bunts had hurt him, and here was Maybelle bleeding, too, even through the bandages that Jigger had put around her head with such a lot of skill. Like he had been a doctor.

It seemed to me to mean something—that the two of them that were wounded were Maybelle and poor Wayne. Jigger and me seemed just to be outsiders, looking in. Wayne and Maybelle were the ones that really counted. And the kid seemed to understand it, too. I was glad to leave before Maybelle's senses came back to her. Jigger followed me out.

There stood the kid and me under the stars, he with his sombrero in his hand.

"God forgive her," Jigger said, very solemn.

I couldn't speak back to him. I was too choked. But I knew that Jigger would never be a real man until he had to ask forgiveness for himself, not for Maybelle.

There you are. I suppose that there is nothing so important as the beginning of how a good man turns crooked. And what had hounded me is that part I had in it—and how much was I to blame? Nobody, I suppose, is very well able to judge me. But anyway, I am mighty glad that at last I have got it all wrote down.

About the Author

Max Brand is the best-known pen name of Frederick Faust, creator of Dr. Kildare, Destry, and many other fictional characters popular with readers and viewers worldwide. Faust wrote for a variety of audiences in many genres. His enormous output, totaling approximately thirty million words or the equivalent of five hundred thirty ordinary books, covered nearly every field: crime, fantasy, historical romance, espionage, Westerns, science fiction, adventure, animal stories, love, war, and fashionable society, big business and big medicine. Eighty motion pictures have been based on his works along with many radio and television programs. For good measure, he also published four volumes of poetry. Perhaps no other author has reached more people in such a variety of different ways.

Born in Seattle in 1892, orphaned early, Faust grew up in the rural San Joaquin Valley of California. At Berkeley he became a student rebel and one-man literary movement, contributing prodigiously to all campus publications. Denied a degree because of unconventional conduct, he embarked on a series of adventures culminating in New York City where, after a period of near starvation, he received simultaneous recognition as a serious poet and successful author of fiction. Later, he traveled widely, making his home in New York, then in Florence, Italy, and finally in Los Angeles.

Once the United States entered the Second World War, Faust abandoned his lucrative writing career and his work as a screenwriter to serve as a war correspondent with the infantry in Italy, despite his fifty-one years and a bad heart. He was killed during a night attack on a hilltop village held by the German army. New books based on magazine serials or unpublished manuscripts or restored versions continue to appear so that, alive or dead, he has averaged a new book every six months for seventy-five years. Beyond this, some work by him is newly reprinted every week of every year in one or another format somewhere in the world. A great deal more about this author and his work can be found in *The Max Brand Companion* (Greenwood Press, 1997) edited by Jon Tuska and Vicki Piekarski. His Website is www.MaxBrandOnline.com.

| Books are produced in the United States using U.S.-based materials | Books are printed using a revolutionary new process called THINKtech™ that lowers energy usage by 70% and increases overall quality | Books are durable and flexible because of Smyth-sewing | Paper is sourced using environmentally responsible foresting methods and the paper is acid-free |

Center Point Large Print
600 Brooks Road / PO Box 1
Thorndike, ME 04986-0001 USA

(207) 568-3717

US & Canada:
1 800 929-9108
www.centerpointlargeprint.com